About the author

J. Collins Kelly is a writer who has been a soldier, trade union representative, engineer and businessman. In recent years, his writing has focused on short stories, of which ***Sting in the Tail*** is his latest collection. Married with two sons, he lives in Ayr, Scotland.

To Cheryl
With best wishes
J. Kelly
21/4/16

STING IN THE TAIL

J.COLLINS KELLY

O p OSWALD
publishing

Contents

1. **The Heist**   1

2. **The Door**   8

3. **The Killer**   12

4. **Heads You Win, Tails You Lose**   18

5. **Jungle Life**   41

6. **The Odyssey of a Misbegotten Soul**   47

7. **The Black Dog**   87

8. **Rescued from P45**   92

9. **Just Cruising Along**   121

1. The Heist

Michael pulled the Jaguar into the lay-by and sat for a moment to regain his composure, then jumped out. That had been one of the fastest drives he had ever done in any car. His heart was still thumping wildly and he could feel his skin tingling with excitement. He stretched out his hands in front of him and saw that they were shaking. Even with the potential danger of what he had just done he had never felt more exhilarated and alive than he did at that moment. The car had performed wonderfully. He stepped back a little from it and looked at its graceful shape. It truly was a thing of beauty; even as it sat there motionless it still radiated movement in every sweeping line and curve of its streamlined body.

Michael's only regret was its colour, in retrospect he should have chosen anything other than white, which he thought made it stand out like a sore thumb from the rest of the traffic almost saying to any passing police patrol car, here I am, come and get me, I'm speeding. Other than that slight niggle it was one of the best handling cars he had ever driven.

Just as he was regaining something approaching normality a battered old Ford car drew up behind him and two rather scruffy looking individuals alighted and approached him, both were smirking broadly.

"Now that's what I call a car," one said.

Michael grinned and nodded to them.

"What's the highest speed you've had it up too, mate?" the taller of them asked.

"Oh about a hundred and ten," Michael replied.

The tall one turned to his blonde companion and

said, "Did you hear that Tom, he has had it up to a hundred and ten," and laughingly added while kicking his car's ropy looking tyre, "Almost as fast as this old bucket."

The blonde one said nothing but just stared at them. Michael started to get an uncomfortable feeling and sensed an air of tension starting to build up.

"Is it auto or manual?" the tall one enquired.

Michael, now feeling distinctly uneasy replied, "It's manual."

He was then just about to say it was time he was off when suddenly he was viciously thumped on the side of his head by the blonde guy who had moved behind him, amazingly he did not fall to the ground, but this was soon rectified when the tall one added his considerable contribution by punching Michael hard on the same area. The blonde one now leaned over Michael saying, "How's that for starters, you rich bugger." He then swung his boot back to kick Michael who put his arms over his face for protection. When the kick came it was mercifully directed at his ribs, the blow took the wind from Michael.

"Give me the bloody keys!" his attacker said.

"They're still in the ignition," Michael replied. "Take the car, just leave me alone."

"Oh so you are giving us the car, thank you so very much," the tall one retorted.

With that he proceeded to kick Michael's body once more, this was quickly followed by the blonde one again entering into the session of gratuitous violence by kicking him three more times, smiling broadly as he did so. Then he got hold of Michael's arm and removed his wristwatch, saying, "And I'll have this."

He was just about to join his co-attacker when he saw Michael was wearing gloves. "You're a right ponce, are you not, wearing gloves, never mind I'll have them."

With that he proceeded to rip the gloves from Michael's hands after which he gave Michael a further hard kick to the chest, he then joined his fellow assailant in the Jaguar and laughingly shouted, "Bye, bye Poncey," as they roared off.

Michael painfully sat up and slipped his hand under his denim jacket and gingerly felt around his chest area to ascertain if he had sustained any broken ribs, thankfully everything seemed to be normal (he had attended a first aid course many years ago). Although he was extremely sore, he was not badly injured. Michael watched as the Jaguar was swiftly driven down the road leaving him with the old Ford, which had in all probability been obtained in the same manner as they had just acquired the Jaguar.

The Good Samaritan

Michael did not want to be associated with the abandoned car just in case it had indeed been stolen and the police were looking for it, so he moved a good distance down the road away from it before attempting to hitch a lift. Quite a few cars passed him by before a kindly truck driver stopped and picked him up.

"You seem to have had a rough time of it mate, are you all right?" were his first words to Michael, "I

3

could see you wincing as you climbed in."

Michael, who was still feeling the effects of his physical and mental trauma could not be bothered to relay all that had happened to him so he merely told the driver that he had fallen down a rocky incline and had lost his haversack and consequently he was now forced to make his way back home.

The driver commiserated with him and said when he was younger he too had been very keen on walking holidays. Michael gave him an amiable smile as if to agree with him, at the same time thinking that of all of the holidays that he would wish to take, a walking one would be the nearest thing to being in hell. The driver asked him if he would like a drink of coffee as he had a flask of it behind Michael's seat. Michael thanked him but, on bending around to retrieve the flask, he soon got a sharp reminder of his painfully bruised ribs that the despicable duo had inflicted on him. He wondered where they now were and what other sickening deeds they had perpetrated in the meanwhile, and also whether the lovely Jaguar was still in one piece. Michael poured out a mug of coffee for himself and the driver, who continued to chat as they proceeded, Michael only pretended to pay attention as he had more important thoughts to occupy his mind.

The Undisputed Evidence

As the truck ascended a particularly steep gradient Michael noticed that the traffic volume had increased substantially, once over the brow of the hill it soon became clear why there was such a build-up of

4

traffic, it was due to a police roadblock. As they slowly moved forward, Michael saw the Jaguar sitting at the side of the road surrounded by a posse of armed policemen - and who should be standing there in handcuffs but the two brutal louts who had attacked him. But for the presence of the truck driver Michael would have shouted out for joy. The traffic ground to a halt and their truck stopped right beside a police officer. Michael rolled down the window.

"What's happening officer?" he asked the policeman.

"Oh just a bank robber we were seeking, but we have him in custody, now please move along."

Michael could not believe his luck. As they slowly passed the roadblock, the blonde character happened to look up and caught sight of Michael looking at him with wide-eyed astonishment. Michael took the opportunity to smile broadly at him and gave him the thumbs up sign. As the blonde villain started to shout and swear at Michael, the policemen misconstrued this as resisting arrest and promptly bundled both muggers into a waiting van. They were still cursing and shouting as they were driven away to the nick.

Michael was euphoric with the outcome of events. Not in his wildest dreams could he have envisaged that there could have been such a justifiably quick result meted out to that abominable vicious pair. The truck driver commented on how much better Michael was looking, and he responded that he felt absolutely wonderful. A short while later he said goodbye to the driver, thanked him most profusely and handed him a ten-pound note. The driver was taken aback by this gesture and initially refused to take it, saying he had been more than happy to help him, but Michael insisted saying that the driver had been of great assistance to him.

Once Michael arrived at his flat he took off his denim jacket and laid it flat on the dining room table which revealed that, sewn all around the inside, was row on row of rectangular pockets in which was stuffed wads of money. This was the same money that Michael had robbed from the bank he held up at gunpoint a short time before he was accosted by those two idiots. It was that same money which had been instrumental in saving him from getting his ribs broken, as the close-packed cash had absorbed and cushioned the impact of the kicks. After joyfully counting his loot, he put a ready meal in the microwave, poured himself a stiff whiskey and settled down to await the evening news on the TV.

It was reported that there had been a hold-up at the County Bank. The robber had been caught on the bank's security system, which clearly showed that he was armed with a pistol (it was a toy) and that he wore a black ski mask and black gloves, and witnesses said that he wore a very distinctive yellow-faced wristwatch. All of these items had been found on an individual who was with another man in the getaway car, a white Jaguar, and both were now under arrest. The car in question had been stolen only a few hours before the robbery from a local car park (fortuitously the silly owner had left the keys in the ignition which saved Michael the bother of having to hot-wire it). A police spokesman said that, although the robber's face could not be seen due to the mask, they had more than enough circumstantial evidence to sustain a conviction. The other man in the Jaguar was assumed to be the getaway driver. The TV reporter asked the policeman if the stolen money had been recovered.

"Not yet, as they must have stashed it away somewhere before we had detained them, but I'm sure the robbers will cooperate and reveal where the money is to help reduce their prison term as this type of crime carries a substantial sentence."

Michael lay back in his chair and cupped his hands behind his head and laughingly said aloud, "Now that's what I call justice, and it could not have happened to a nicer pair."

2. The Door

One day I decided to paint the front door of my flat; a task I initially thought could be completed expeditiously and would dry to a nice high-gloss, pleasing finish that would enhance the flat entrance. I remembered that I had a large tin of paint stored in my garden shed, which had been surplus to my requirements when I was doing some decorating the previous year. However, on opening it I was almost overcome by its rancid foul smell, which could best be described as a compound mixture of rotten whale blubber intermixed with raw sewage, with just a hint of pig's urine. Visually, it resembled a collection of pulverized intestines. The reason why the paint smelt and looked so awful was that, in all probability when it had became frozen (during one of the coldest winters we have had in the past thirty years), this had caused the paint to chemically separate into its constituent parts, then when it unfroze the result was a congealed mess with a highly repugnant odour.

At first I was a little bit apprehensive about using the paint, but due to my impecunious position - and my Calvinistic Scottish upbringing of always being advised to never waste anything - I took the decision, which at the time seemed appropriate for someone suffering penury, to go ahead and use the substance. It was however a hasty and ill-advised choice which I was later to deeply regret.

I will forgo fully recounting the convoluted and messy process of applying the slimy gelatinous substance to the door - suffice it to say that, by the time I had completed the energy sapping task, my olfactory senses were totally overwhelmed by the stomach churning stench, which effected not only my throat but also my eyes, even although I was wearing both a face mask and goggles. I placated myself by thinking of how much money I was saving.

I had presumed that the resurrected paint would in all probably take slightly longer to dry than normal, as would its nauseous smell in dissipating, but as the hours progressed into days and the days into weeks, the intensity of the smell did not diminish one iota. I tried placing an electric fan heater in close proximity to the offending door in the hope of hastening the drying-out process, but this only assisted the abominable smell to permeate even further into the flat. I then tried spraying it with numerous cans of scented aerosol, but this, once again, only aggravated the situation. I even attempted keeping the windows wide open for a protracted period (not an inconsiderable thing to do in the middle of an Edinburgh winter), but still without any tangible success.

It had become obvious that, after living with this intolerable situation for a month, something drastic had to be done, as the 'Paint' appeared to be in a permanent destabilized state and - if I were to avoid that same fate - I would have to remove the source of my acute discomfort. So I decided to take the bull by the horns and finalize the whole affair. I got my trusty screwdriver, removed the door completely, wrapped it in masses of cling film and made my way very cautiously and exhaustedly down the stairwell with it. While doing so I met a few of my neighbours who, when they got within smelling distance of me,

9

pressed themselves against the wall and pinched their noses. I was unsure whether they thought the smell emanated from the door or me.

On reaching the back garden I placed the door on the ground, obtained a quantity of kerosene from my garden shed, sprinkled a liberal amount of it over the door and joyfully set it alight, standing well back as it exploded into flames. During these past weeks, I had come to hate that door with a vengeance, so it was with a high degree of satisfaction that I watched it being consumed. The flames rose higher and higher and the smell got stronger and stronger. The flames contained a peculiar pattern of multi-coloured hues as the various chemicals were exposed to the searing heat. Watching the conflagration, I saw a seagull fly through the periphery of the dense billowing smoke and, within seconds, it had dropped dead, asphyxiated at my feet. It was brutal testimony to just how noxious the paint chemicals were. I picked the dead bird up and gave it a Viking send off by tossing it onto the funeral pyre.

As I happily stood there enjoying the bonfire, I suddenly saw some embers fly from the fire and land on my hut roof, which of course being covered in tarry felt immediately caught fire. Panic stricken, I rushed back upstairs for a bucket of water, but by the time I had retraced my steps most of the water had spilled from the bucket and my hut was well and truly ablaze. The next thing I heard was the sound of sirens as the fire brigade (called by my ever-vigilant neighbours) arrived accompanied by the police, who promptly sealed-off both ends of the street, which attracted a substantial number of on- lookers. By the time the firemen had unravelled their hoses, both the door and the hut were no more. I stood there totally dumbfounded that a simple task of painting a door could have instigated such an outcome. Rather than saving money by using that so-called paint, it had cost me an arm and a leg in purchasing aerosols, electricity for the heater, a new door, not forgetting another tin of paint, and my shed with all of its contents - that incidentally included my new bicycle which had been a recent birthday present from my parents. In addition to which, my previously friendly neighbours now give me a wide-berth whenever they see me coming, as they now considered me to be a foul-smelling arsonist. The Police interviewed and charged me, which required engaging a lawyer to represent me in court. My case comes up next week. I also had a visit from a representative of the Royal Society for the Protection of Birds, and that organization is also considering prosecuting me. After the calamity of the day had died down, I retired to my bedroom with a bottle of whiskey to drown my sorrows when my eye alighted on an old wall plaque that my maternal grandmother had given me many years ago, on which was inscribed "Waste not want not". I swiftly removed it from the wall and threw it in the garbage bin.

3. The Killer

Richard ran his hand along the camouflaged barrel of his German Smitenhoffer TR 373 rifle which had served him well over these last five years, never having failed in even the most daunting and sometimes very inclement conditions in which he was sometimes required to operate. Richard had served with the SAS in numerous parts of the world, primarily as a sniper and had killed many times, in such diverse places as Bosnia, Iraq and Afghanistan. To the best of his knowledge, he had always killed outright, with one shot, never merely wounding any of his allocated targets. He always aimed at the head, which was of course far more difficult than a body shot. So far, he had never missed. The first time he had killed, it totally shattered his whole being and he found it very difficult even to sleep. The second time, it was a little bit less stressful, but he was still troubled by what he was required to do. By the third killing, he had almost become inured to it and thereafter it did not bother him at all. He had formed a hard, impenetrable psychological protective shield around his conscience and forced himself to view those individuals he was ordered to kill as merely "Targets". This afforded him the ability to remain emotionally detached from what he had to do.

Being in the SAS, as far as Richard was concerned, had been one of his better decisions in life. He enjoyed the lifestyle with its attendant dangers when on active duty (which was more often than the general public were aware of). Killing the "Enemy" never bothered him, as he had further coerced himself into taking the dispassionate view that his "Target" had obviously done something heinous, or was about to, and that the only way to stop them was with a well-placed bullet.

The basic training regime in the SAS was very tough - one could almost say cruel. Often, one had to remain hidden in a camouflaged foxhole for protracted periods, waiting for your target to arrive at your designated position. This was not too bad if the weather happened to be good, but more often than not it rained, which slowly, sometimes not so slowly, filled up your hiding place. This left you sitting in a gradually rising pool of muddy water, which soon had you shivering with cold. No matter, you were still expected to remain where you were. This situation became even more fraught when darkness fell, and worse still when you needed to heed a call of nature. Still, you had to remain hidden. Failure to do so would mean you had forfeited your chance to be accepted and you would unceremoniously be tufted out of the training course.

Richard had risen to the rank of RSM and had completed eighteen years with the regiment. He had been decorated many times for bravery and outstanding work. Often, he would operate on his own behind enemy lines, cut off from contact with his comrades - sometimes for weeks at a time - patiently waiting for the right opportunity to take that one shot at his assigned target. Having done so, he would extract himself from the locale without any outside help.

The first thing you had to do was get rid of your weapon, then blend in with the populace, dressed like the rest of the community. Wearing a uniform under indigenous clothes would not give you any protection because, if you were captured, you would almost certainly be shot whether you were wearing one or not. More likely, you would also be tortured, before being summarily executed. So, to be a member of the SAS, you needed to be extremely tough both physically and psychologically.

When Richard retired from the regiment, he truly missed his comrades, who on many an occasion had saved his bacon. Equally, at other times, he had saved theirs. Each member of the regiment viewed the SAS not just as a section within the army, but something more akin to a family where everyone looked out for everyone else. It was a very close bond indeed, often cemented with blood and shared danger of the highest order.

Richard had tried quite a few jobs but was always restless and dissatisfied. Then, one night, as he was watching a movie about a hired killer, the thought suddenly came to him - why not start up a business for people who require to have a problem in their life removed by someone willing to do the killing for them. Richard had always thought that starting and running a business would be difficult and bristling with problems, but in his specialised type of business this was far from the truth. He was amazed how many people required his particular services. Within a short while, the enterprise became firmly established, most of it simply by word of mouth.

Now, after five years of killing, he was calling a halt, as his knees were starting to become stiff with arthritis. Worse still, it was also beginning to affect his trigger finger, so he was now on his last operational outing.

The target lived in a hilly and dense wooded area. Once at the location, Richard settled himself down on a high vantage point and waited for the target to arrive, as he was advised he habitually did between eleven and twelve. Richard checked his rifle, operating the bolt back and forth a few times. He loaded the magazine into it and operated the bolt once again, as he put a round into the chamber and checked that the safety was locked on. Now, all he had to do was wait. This was the time that Richard truly hated. He would much rather get it all over with as quickly as possible, more especially as this was to be his last killing.

Richard took out his binoculars and made a swift survey of the area, then set them down on the grass nearby and continued his vigil. About half an hour later, he happened to look down at the binoculars, and observed that a spider had almost completed spinning a web across one of its lenses. As he watched, a fly became entangled in it. A spider darted out and stung the fly into submission, then wrapped it up in silk thread and dragged it away. Richard could not help but compare what the spider had just done with what he was about to do and thought nostalgically that in the end death will also claim the spider, as it would eventually claim him.

The weather was nicely calm, so there would be no need to allow for wind-drift on the bullet. He selected a mark point on the ground where a small branch lay about forty yards away. This would be where he would kill the target. Another fifteen minutes passed. Richard heard the distinct sound of breaking twigs, signalling the approach of his intended victim.

Very slowly, he brought his rifle up to the aim position and just as slowly eased off the safety catch. He peered through the high-powered telescopic gun sight. The target was slowly making his way towards him. Maybe because it was to be the last time he would have to kill, he could feel a rush of adrenaline pass through him and a slight twinge of nervousness, something he had not experienced for a long, long time.

The target was now only a few moments away from eternity. Richard brought the crosshairs of the 'scope onto the victim's head and willed the target to take that last couple of steps forward. Suddenly, a twig broke under the weight of Richard's foot. The target looked up in his direction. Richard's reflexes reacted instantly. The bullet tore through the victim's scull, completely shattering and pulverizing the brain tissue. Death was instantaneous.

Richard had thought that he would, as usual, feel detached and dispassionate regarding this last killing, but strangely he did not. He did something he had never done before - take a closer look at his handiwork. Usually, he left this part of the operation to others. Bending down to pick up his binoculars, he saw that his fellow killer was still there, so he got a blade of grass and slowly teased the spider from its resting place and put it gently onto the ground. He watched as it scuttled away into the safety of the undergrowth. Then slowly, he descended the rocky mound and approached the target.

The shot had been near perfect. The entry point was just above the left eye, which obviously meant instant death. Richard put his hand into his old Barbour jacket and fished out his mobile phone. He rang out a number and merely said, "That's it done, you can pick him up. He is lying at the north side of the mound."

He looked down at the stag. It was a truly magnificent specimen with ten point antlers. Even in death, it still looked imperial. Some people thought that culling was cruel, but if they could only see the devastation that starvation brings to a herd when it become too large, they would soon change their mind.

Richard took one last look at the beautiful highland landscape, then slung his rifle across his shoulders and started on the long walk back to his Land Rover.

4. Heads You Win Tails You Lose

"Bob, that's the coffee ready."

Bob wiped his brow and pulled off his facemask. "Okay Vic," he shouted, and then climbed down the ladder.

"I'm more than ready for a break," he thought, "and I don't think I should have tackled a job like this on such a warm day."

'This job' was stripping old wallpaper from walls of the toilet at his brother Vic's holiday home in Lunel in southern France. Initially, it had seemed such an easy task, which he hoped to complete in a very short space of time. But once he got started, he found that this was very far from being so. There had been so many pieces of wallpaper plastered one on top of another over many, many decades that the end result felt as if he was removing cardboard. It was hard sweaty work. Bob had initially thought he might do the whole task in a few hours. Now, he reappraised this time scale to possibly two days.

A day and a half later, Bob was still hard at work on the north-facing wall and finding that, when he removed some very stubborn pieces of wallpaper, often a large chunk of plaster came with them, thus requiring additional remedial work before he could start painting. Eventually, he was working on the very last piece of extremely thick paper, which was resisting all of his muscular attempts to remove it. He decided the best method was to soak it with warm water, which he hoped would permeate the individual layers - a method he had used in his Victorian flat in Edinburgh.

He joined Vic and his wife Jennifer for a well-earned coffee break, during which time Vic asked Bob to leave off working on the walls for a while and join them for a swim. Bob being Bob said he would rather finish what he had started and complete the task.

As Bob entered the room to restart his work, he noticed that the wallpaper had started to peel away from its vice-like grip on the wall. His attention was drawn to a square-shaped central section which was still holding on tenaciously.

Bob mounted the ladder. Once near to the problem piece of wallpaper, he could see that there appeared to be something underneath. He quickly scraped away the remainder of the paper, which revealed a square area of cast iron with four rusty bolts, one at each corner.

He looked at it for a few moments, wondering what it could possibly be. Then he noticed in the very centre of it was a raised section. Bob scraped away at this and soon he could see it was the imprint of an eagle, which he assumed was some kind of company logo.

Bob continued to work away at the iron bolts, but it was tiring work in such high temperatures. At one point, he considered just painting over it, as in all probability, behind the intractable cover, would be just an old water cut-off valve. But Bob's perfectionist nature would never counter that easy solution, nor would it satisfy his usual insatiable curiosity. Consequently, he continued to do battle with the bolts. Eventually, one after the other, each bolt sheared off and he gingerly removed the cover.

What he saw in that dark opening was not some ancient domestic plumbing but an encrusted piece of dirty black cloth covering something round. He was just about to insert his hand to retrieve the object, when suddenly he had an uneasy feeling about what he was looking at.

Restraining his curiosity, he descended the steps and looked around for something with which to extract the mystery object. He found a pair of coal tongs in the sitting room fireplace. Armed with these, he again approached the object. Slowly and cautiously, he pulled it outward. Once it was at the edge of the hole, Bob let it rest there for a moment, unsure whether he should place his bare hands on it.

Bob studied the odd-shaped thing for several moments. His innate curiosity was beginning to get the better of his reticence. He estimated that the object must weigh at least one-and-a-half kilos, going by its resistance when he was pulling it by the tongs to extract it. He took hold of the dirty object, keeping it at arm's length, and navigated himself precariously down the ladder. In the kitchen, he placed the object on a wooden chair. Once again, he pondered what he was looking at and why he was so reluctant to remove its dirty cloth.

The reason why he was so reticent became clear when he noticed how similar the shape of the object was to that of a human skull. Recoiling in horror, Bob realized not only what the entity might be but also that he had made physical contact with it. He ran over to the sink and washed his hands vigorously. It was only when he was drying his hands that he began to feel foolish in his reaction to what he had found.

Obviously, whatever was concealed beneath the rag had been sealed up for well over a hundred years. Consequently, any contaminant would have ceased to be effective a long time ago. Nevertheless, Bob was very circumspect when he started to remove the dirty cloth from the object.

A Blast from The Past

Even as Bob uncovered the very first portion of what lay under the cloth, it was abundantly clear that he had been correct in his assumption. Within a few moments, the skull was fully revealed. Uncovered, it did not seem so unnerving. In fact, it reminded him of his childhood days when his parents used to take him to the Kelvingrove museum in Glasgow, where ancient skulls were on display. This skull had that same polished appearance. Its teeth were badly worn down and decayed, signifying that the person had been old when death occurred, possibly in his sixties.

"Why did I assume it to be male?" Bob thought. "It could just as well be female. Either way, after such a long time, what did it matter?"

At that point in his ruminations, a call of nature required him to revisit the toilet. Suddenly, he heard an almighty scream. He rushed to the kitchen and was confronted with Jennifer, standing there with open-mouthed astonishment, looking down at the skull.

"What on earth is that?" she shouted.

"It's a skull."

"I can see that, but what is it doing in my kitchen?"

"I found it in the toilet," Bob replied.

"You mean it floated up from within the bowl?"

"No," said Bob. "I found it behind a cast iron cavity in the wall."

"What cast iron cavity?" Jennifer asked.

"Come with me and I'll show you."

Once back in the toilet room, Bob gestured to the hole in the wall. "It was hidden behind the old wallpaper."

Jennifer grimaced. "You mean to tell me that horrible thing was there all the time we have been using this room?"

"Well, it couldn't do you any harm."

"You wouldn't say that if you had found one in your toilet," Jennifer retorted.

"Maybe you'd be right, Jennifer, especially if it was the toilet in my flat in Edinburgh. The building is so old, I would not be surprised if Sweeny Todd had lived there."

They returned to the kitchen. Jennifer asked Bob what he intended to do with the skull.

"I'll tell you what I'm going to do with it," he replied. "Nothing. It's not my house. So, it's not my responsibility - it's yours and Vic's. It's probably a leftover from the French Revolution. Just think. All this time you and Vic were living here, you didn't know you had an aristocrat's head for company."

"Seriously, Bob - what are we to do with it?" said Jennifer. "Should we inform the police?"

"I could quite easily put it back where I got it and paper over it again," said Bob, "How about that?"

"Stop it, Bob," she retorted. "This is serious. We will have to inform the authorities."

"Yes, I know. Now, where do you keep your telephone directory? I suppose I'll have to look under the 'lost and found' section."

Jennifer gave him a withering look and told him to get on with it. Just at that juncture, they heard the door open, as Vic came into the room, saying, "What's keeping you, Jennifer? I told you the sun cream was in the bathroom cupboard."

Bob and Jennifer turned to him.

"Why are you two looking at me like that?" he asked.

Jennifer pursed her lips and pointed at the skull.

Vic went over to the skull and picked it up. "You have surpassed yourself this time, Bob. This is really very life-like, even down to the dirty old rag. Where did you manage to get it?"

"It's real, Vic," said Jennifer. "Bob found it in the toilet."

"What - in the bowl?"

"Oh, not again," Bob exclaimed, "No, Vic - in the wall."

"What wall?"

"Where I was working," said Bob.

Vic looked at the skull he was holding. "You mean to tell me this is real?"

With that, he let the skull fall onto the floor, and ran to the sink to wash his hands saying, "Good God, it's real…"

Bob thought it time for him to interject some calm into the situation. "The skull is, at the very least, over a hundred years old," he said, authoritatively. "So I don't think there is any possibility of catching something from it."

"But it's gross - it was someone's head," Vic replied.

"Yes, it was," said Bob, "but don't you think it has very nice teeth?"

Jennifer scowled. "Stop it, Bob."

Rub a Dub Dub, One Man and His Tub

Once Vic had come down to the lower end of his panic scale, he said, "We will have to let the police know what we have found."

"That's exactly what I was just saying to Bob," said Jennifer. "Vic, pick it up, and I'll wrap it in this old newspaper."

"Not on your Nelly," Vic replied, as he moved further away from the skull.

Jennifer looked at Bob. "Please," she said.

"Oh, all right," Bob told her, "but give me the newspaper."

Bob walked to where the skull had fallen. He wrapped the newspaper around it and picked it. "It has landed in some dog's poo on the floor," he exclaimed, and added, "Well, don't look in my direction. You're the only ones who have been out this morning."

Both Jennifer and Vic checked the soles of their shoes. "Sorry," said Vic.

"Well, we can't show it to anyone looking like this, can we?" said Jennifer.

She suggested that they put it in a bucket of water and give it a good rinse.

"And I suppose that will be another nice job for me to do," said Bob.

"Yes, please," said Jennifer.

Bob shrugged his shoulders and proceeded with the task. "This is the first, and I hope the last, time I'll be washing a French person's head."

"Get on with it, slave," called Vic, from the safety of the other side of the room.

"Yes, oh mighty fearless one," Bob retorted, and then retired to the old scullery at the back of the house.

"Open Nice and Wide Please"

Bob finished rinsing the skull, then removed it from the bucket and sat it on the newspaper. He noticed that something was logged in the back of the skull's mouth. It looked about one-and-a-half inches in diameter and about quarter of an inch thick, and was encrusted with dirt. Bob tried to prise it out with an old spoon, but without success. He took the skull back into the kitchen, where he could get a much better look at it, and showed Jennifer and Vic what he had found.

"I'll get something from my tool box," said Vic.

Jennifer, knowing how few DIY tools Vic actually possessed, offered to sacrifice one of her kitchen tongs to enable Bob to extract what was in the skull's mouth. It was but a small concession to help satisfy her increasing curiosity.

Bob obtained a table lamp from the front room. He directed its light into the skull's cavernous mouth and proceeded to probe at the mystery object. It was so firmly lodged that it took Bob some considerable time to loosen and retrieve it. Once out for all to see, it appeared to be was some kind of medal, as it was obviously too big to be a coin. Bob retraced his steps to the scullery and the trusty water bucket. With a fresh supply of water, plus the help of an old toothbrush, he soaked and brushed the accumulated detritus of the past hundred years off of the object. He received his second surprise that day when he observed the glint of gold.

Even if what he was holding had no value other than its intrinsic weight, it was still worth a pretty penny at today's gold prices. But if it also was of some historical or archaeological significance, then they might be on to a real winner.

Bob rushed back to the kitchen and proclaimed the good news. Vic moved over from the far side of the room and suggested that the skull, even on its own, might be of important significance. Consequently, the sum total of what they had discovered could be quite rewarding.

"Correction - what you meant to say was what Bob discovered," Bob interjected.

Vic sighed. "Oh, all right. What Bob discovered…in our house."

All Hail the Emperor

Jennifer reminded Bob that he had yet to make the telephone call to the police.

"Hold on a moment," said Vic. "If we call the police, they will take it away for examination and you know what the French are like. They will tie it up for years in red tape and we will never get to know what it is and more importantly not accrue any financial benefit. Think about that."

They all looked at each other for a few moments.

"At one of these fancy diplomatic dinner parties I attended recently," said Jennifer, "I was introduced to someone who worked at the Louvre. Now, what was his name…oh, yes - I remember. It was a professor Klinhoff. He said if I ever needed his help, I was to get in touch with him. I remember thinking at the time, that will be the day. I'm sure I have his card somewhere." She ran off to find it.

Meanwhile, Bob and Vic continued to closely examine the medal. There was still a considerable amount of encrusted dirt clinging to both sides of the object. Bob asked Vic to give him his Swiss army knife and proceeded to slowly and gingerly pick off minute pieces of matter. Gradually, letters started to appear - first "N", then "A", followed by "P", swiftly followed by the letter "O".

"Vic," said Bob, breathlessly, "I think we have struck gold in more than one way. I'm sure this is going to spell out 'Napoleon'."

Jennifer returned. "I took the liberty of phoning the professor. He was extremely excited with what I told him, in particular the artefact that was in the mouth of the skull. But he advised me to contact the police. I protested that would only complicate matters, as the gendarmerie tend to be more than a little ponderous when required to handle anything that might be of French archaeological importance. I said, 'Surely the skull would be of no interest to them, as it was well over a hundred years old.' He replied, 'they would not just accept your word for that. Any human remains that are found, even if they

27

appear to be very old, must in the first instance be reported to the police. That's the law. It will then go to their forensic department for analysis to determine its age, and if it's as old as you think, it will be returned to you.' With regard to the medal, he was very keen to examine it, but once again said that it would also have to be reported to the police as it could possibly be implicated in a crime, as the skull and the medal might not be time compatible."

"Damn," said Vic and Bob simultaneously, on hearing this.

Bob continued to minutely pick away at the encrusted dirt covering the medal. Just as he had surmised, he soon exposed the word "Napoleon". After further work on the reverse side, an image of the Emperor emerged. He continued to clean and burnish it. Vic started to search the Internet for information regarding Napoleonic medals. After an hour, he shouted, "Eureka" and started to sing, "we're in the money…we're in the money…"

Once he had come back down to earth, he explained his shout of joy. "It seems that old 'Boney' issued only five of these medals, which were given for totally outstanding courage and valour. One is now in the Louvre, one in the Metropolitan Museum in New York, and three have been missing. It appears we have found one of the missing ones. How about that?" He added, smiling, "that's not all the good news. When the Metropolitan bought theirs in the late 1930s, they paid a whopping one million dollars for it. So, taking intervening years of inflation into consideration, we have acquired not a golden medal but a nice golden hen which will lay us some very

28

lucrative eggs, if only we can keep our hands on the hen."

Friends in High Places

Reluctantly, Vic made the call to the local gendarmerie and relayed what they had found. He informed them that he thought the skull was quite ancient, to which he got the officious reply, "We will be the best judge of that monsieur."

They said they would call in about an hour's time. Vic hung up the receiver with a heavy heart. "Now, all the usual French officious nonsense will start," he said, and added, "The medal, I'm sure, is worth a very large sum of money. I think we should take some precautions with it."

"You surely don't think any of the police would steal it," said Jennifer.

"If the medal is the genuine article, it's worth a fortune," Vic replied, "and with that sort of money, who knows what can happen? All I'm saying is let's do something which will clearly demonstrate that the medal was in our possession."

Bob suggested that they photograph the medal while each of them held it in one hand, with the daily newspaper clearly showing the date in the other. Having done this, they heard the sound of a car, which they assumed was the police arriving to pick up the skull and medal. But on looking out of the window, Vic saw that it was the Mayor. Without waiting to explain what he was about to do, Vic rushed out and waylaid the Mayor, who was on his way to the town hall.

Jennifer and Bob dashed over to the window and

observed Vic having an animated conversation with the Mayor, who had a look of astonishment on his face. Vic was obviously informing him of their mysterious find. After a few more moments, Vic reappeared with a slightly mystified-looking Mayor in tow. "Now, your Honour, I would like you to assert that these two objects - namely this human skull and this gold medal - are in my possession. If I write out this affidavit, would you please sign that you have witnessed that these same articles are in my house on this recorded date and time."

"With pleasure, Monsieur Drummond," said the Mayor, and duly signed the paper. Vic thanked him and offered him a glass of wine. The Mayor refused, saying he was in a hurry, but would be glad to do so on another occasion. He asked Vic to keep him informed regarding the skull and, in particular, the medal.

Just as he was about to leave, they heard a knock at the door. On opening it, Vic found the officious face of the local gendarme staring back at him. The policeman said nothing but continued to stare. Probably this was his silly technique to hopefully intimidate people.

"I suppose you are here regarding the skull?" said Vic.

"Of course, of course - why else do you think I am here?" the little martinet replied aggressively. "I'll also require you to hand over the medal. Now, show me where it is."

He rudely pushed past Vic and entered the hallway and then uninvited into the kitchen. Vic would have brought the little ballerina up sharp but for the fact of

30

the medal. He did not want to say or do anything which might be recorded as unhelpful behaviour and jeopardise his legitimacy of ownership.

Vic swiftly followed the gendarme, who announced his presence in a loud voice. It was only at that point that the Mayor, who'd had his back to the doorway, turned around. As soon as the policeman recognised the Mayor, all of his blustering behaviour evaporated and he reverted to a stuttering apology for having interrupted.

"Not at all," said the Mayor. "Just make sure you record everything and keep it safe for my friend Monsieur Drummond."

The gendarme, now in full subservient mode, assured the Mayor that he would do everything meticulously. The Mayor departed and the suitably chastened policeman politely requested the skull and medal. He made his way out, but not before Vic informed him that he and Bob were lawyers and should he need any legal advice regarding the law surrounding archaeological artefacts, he was to feel free to give them a call.

Once the gendarme had gone, Vic said, "I think we can now rest easy as to any possibility of the medal going astray after that fortuitous meeting with the Mayor and our pep talk to that little pipsqueak."

Five days passed without any word from the gendarmerie. It looked like the little policeman was taking his revenge. It was time to use the big stick on him. Vic dialled the Mayor's office and had a quiet word with him about the slow progress of information about the skull and medal. Half an hour later, Vic got a call from the little gendarme who had just received word from the laboratory. It seemed that the skull was over the statute of limitations and thus was too old for them to start an investigation.

"And the medal?" Vic asked.

"Ah - that is a different matter," the gendarme replied. "It is something of national importance, so we will be holding onto it for further assessment."

"And what does that mean?" asked Vic.

Mr. Plod replied, "It means, Monsieur, that it will be kept for further assessment. The matter is now closed." With that he put down the phone.

A Policeman's Lot is Not a Happy One

Vic was livid as he raced out of the house and headed for the police station to confront that little dictatorial bumpkin.

By the time he'd reached the station, his temper had not abated one iota, but being a pragmatist, Vic knew that little Mr. Officious would use any excuse to thwart his endeavours to repossess the medal. So he contained his anger and quietly asked for the officer in charge.

Vic was deliberately left waiting for some time. When the lieutenant duly appeared, Vic disarmingly smiled at him and said, "I think, Monsieur, you have misinterpreted a point of law regarding my medal."

The little gendarme looked back at Vic with a dictatorial stare and relied, "I am addressed as Lieutenant, not Monsieur, and the medal has yet to be assessed as to whether it belongs to the state or you. I'm not in the habit of making mistakes regarding the law, so good day, Monsieur."

With that, he waved his hand to indicate the exit door and was about to walk away, when Vic (with stoic calm that surprised even himself) said, "One moment, Lieutenant. The point of law with regard to this matter does not need to be redefined, as it was clearly set out in the statute books in 1811 by Napoleon himself. I will delineate for you what that law says, and I quote. Amendment 21, article 5, subsection 2 of the statutes unequivocally states that, on the acquisition of any property, the new owner is deemed to possess not only the building and its defined ground, but each and every article found therein, unquote."

Earlier, Vic had accessed Google and obtained a modicum of information pertaining to French property rights. The rest he had just made up. He'd found, by experience, that if you spout legalistic jargon with conviction - especially if your audience is aware that you are a lawyer - it tends to be believed. So, he continued by saying, "I now formally make an *ex cathedra* injunction, in the presence of these witnessing officers, that you hand over the medal to me right now."

The disputatious gendarme still prevaricated, saying, "I have only your word for that, and you could be mistaken."

Vic now used the last weapon in his armoury, which he knew would make this little twit jump to attention and immediately comply with his request.

"You have now made it abundantly clear, Lieutenant," he said, "that you intend to flout the law, the very law you were sworn to uphold and defend, which leaves me no alternative but to report your

33

indictable behaviour to the Mayor."

The effect was immediate on the pernickety little authoritarian, not only in his facial expression but also his body language. He jumped into his ever-ready subservient persona at the sound of his lord and master's name being used. Smiling broadly he said, "Now, now, monsieur - there is no need for the Mayor to be involved in such a trifling matter. As you rightly say, the law is the law and we must always bow to its demands."

With a glance at one of the on-looking policemen, he snapped an order for him to retrieve the medal from the security room.

On leaving the police station clutching the hard won medal, Vic knew he had made an enemy of this little local Napoleon. He felt he would have to make plans in the near future to have him quietly removed from Lunel to some other far-flung police district, just as soon as he had time to arrange an appointment with his friend the Mayor.

Vic had been so engrossed in verbal combat that he had completely forgotten about the skull when he left the police station. Retracing his steps to retrieve it, he met a young gendarme running towards him holding said skull.

"You forgot this, Monsieur," said the policeman breathlessly, and handed the uncovered object to Vic.

A passing motorist was so astonished at seeing a policeman handing a human skull to a man in the street that he collided with the car in front. The gendarme walked over to the scene of the accident and took out his little black book.

Now that both artefacts were once again safely back in their hands, Vic, Bob and Jennifer set to work with a vengeance to obtain as much information as they could about their legitimacy and right to sell the skull and more importantly the gold medal.

Vic's legal comments to Mr. Plod had been partially correct, but only partially. In the final analysis, the Institute of National Heritage would have the final word. The Institute demanded possession of the artefacts while the decision as to who was the rightful owner was being adjudicated.

If a decision was made in their favour, the repercussions would be tremendous for each of them. Their whole life would change out of all recognition. So, with that thought uppermost in their mind, every spare moment was spent writing, emailing, phoning and generally pestering the life out of that august French establishment.

A year later, they received a letter asking them to present themselves at the Institute so that they could have a final and definitive opportunity to state their case before the academy directors, who would cross-examine them and consider their evidence to be regarded as the rightful owners of the skull and the Napoleonic medal.

Once they arrived at the Institute they were ushered into an anteroom, where they were served refreshments.

"This is all very nice," said Jennifer, "but I wish they had seen us straight away, as I can feel my legs starting to shake."

Vic and Bob put on their best interpretation of stoic manliness, but in reality both felt like they needed the toilet.

About half an hour later, a door opened. A smartly dressed tall man approached.

"Mademoiselle, Messieurs," he said, and gestured towards the open door.

An Irishwoman and two Scotsmen walked towards their fate.

The Inquisition

The interview room was truly gigantic - of neoclassical design, its ceiling at least twenty foot high. The walls were predominately white and hung with heavy gilt framed portraits. The door surrounds and ornate cornice work were covered in gold leaf. The effect was intimidating.

At the far end of the room was a long oak table covered in a blue cloth, behind which sat four men and one woman on high-backed chairs. The three hopefuls made the long walk towards them. They were welcomed by the woman sitting in the middle. The visitors assumed she was the chairperson. This was confirmed as she addressed them.

"During this past year," she said, "you have bombarded us with every conceivable form of communication regarding the skull and Napoleonic medal which you found at Lunel. Your only response to our numerous detailed replies was to send us even more convoluted and elaborated enquiries. This has got to stop, as we have other more important things to attend to. That is why the directors of the Institute asked you here, so you could clearly define once and for all why you think the skull and medal are your property. Now, would one of you like to begin?"

With a start like that, the chances of them being granted possession of the skull and medal looked doomed from the outset. Vic stood.

"Madame Chair," he said, "all I can say is we are sorry if we took up so much of your time, but if we hadn't done so, you would not have given us this opportunity to meet you today, face to face. I feel that the reasons the Institute have given us are not just or reasonable. The artefacts were found on my property and, as I have previously pointed out to you, your decision to keep these items flies in the face of Napoleonic law statutes. I refer you to my later dated 19th January."

The directors started to talk amongst themselves. Finally, Madame Chair said, "What you have told us today is something we were unaware of. So, we will take a short break while your correspondence is located and checked. The usher will show you to another room while we discuss the point you have raised."

While enjoying the very welcome interruption they probed each other for their reaction to the inquisition.

"When that old dear started to take a strip off of us, I thought we had lost," said Jennifer, "but now I'm not too sure."

"It's unbelievable that they did not know that particular point of law regarding the rights of possession," said Vic, "and did not bother to read my letter which clearly pointed it out."

37

Bob, on the other hand, took a more philosophical view.

"I think that possibly two directors could be on our side."

"As far as I'm concerned, this type of meeting is usually a waste of time, as everything has already been decided," said Vic.

After half an hour, they were recalled to the meeting.

The trio scanned the faces of the assembled directors for any indication of whether their arguments for retaining the skull and medal had been successful or not, but the directors were well versed in hiding their feelings.

Madame Chair spoke. "We have read your letter containing the Napoleonic reference and studied the relevant amendment. We voted whether to accept your supplication or not. I now have to inform you that, on a vote of three to two, it has been decided to acknowledge that you are the rightful owner of the artefacts found at 9 Place De Hotel, Deville 33467 Lunel. However, there is a caveat - that being, should you decide to sell either or both of these artefacts, you will only do so as long as they remain within the boundaries of France. I now ask if you are in agreement with these terms and are willing to sign a deposition to that effect."

The supplicants looked at each other with startled delight. After the long battle of attrition they had finally succeeded.

Vic smiled at the directors and said, "Thank you, thank you, thank you!"

"I take that to mean that you accept the

conditions?" said Madame Chair.

"I'm sorry," Vic replied. "Yes, yes, of course we do."

The Rewards

Two months later, and after a prolonged tussle with the Louvre over the exact amount they were willing to pay, a figure of ten million euros was agreed for the "Lunel Twins" as the media had crassly christened the skull and medal.

Vic and Jennifer did not fully retire, but intermittently continued to teach civil rights law at home and abroad. Jennifer published a best-selling book on international human rights entitled *The Subjugation of Modern Women.* Vic became an associate professor and a renowned photographer. They also purchased a large mansion in the district of Rathgar in Dublin. Bob retired as soon as he was in receipt of his share of the sale of the artefacts. He sold his flat in Edinburgh and bought a villa in Spain and a town house in Paris. He became a full-time artist and his paintings are exhibited in London, Paris and New York. He and his partner Dawn spend most of their time in Paris, where Dawn published her best-selling second book *Life in Paris from an American Point of View.*

If perchance you are in Paris and visit the Louvre, there is a very special room where the skull and medal are exhibited. There you will see a plaque placed beside them, indicating that a Mr. Bob Drummond discovered them in a small village called Lunel. All of this was made possible by the medal's tenuous link to Napoleon, whom they all totally abhorred. Yet every anniversary of the discovery of that medal, no matter what part of the world they are in, they all raise a glass in salutation to the emperor saying, "To Napoleon, the murdering little fart."

Footnotes:
For those of you who are still wondering if Vic achieved his ambition of having the little gendarme moved from Lunel to another location, the answer is yes. The Mayor was instrumental in getting him transferred to the police K9 training establishment in the Pyrenees, where his talent for giving orders was more fully appreciated by the resident trainees.

With regard to the skull, no direct connection was established between it and the gold medal. However, a more detailed inspection of the skull at a later date revealed the name Joseph Guillotine inscribed inside the jaw. This was the name of the French physician who in 1789 recommended his invention as a less painful means of execution and which ironically was later used to remove his own head in 1814.

5. Jungle Life

The raucous sound of a police siren dragged Stewart back into the harsh reality of his life. He had been dreaming about his boyhood days when his future course in life seemed so settled and assured, when his father had been alive and with whom he shared a very close relationship. But all that had changed when his father suddenly died. The effect on both him and his mother was profound. He lost all interest in his academic studies, which up until that point indicated that he was university material. Now that potential bright future had lost all meaning for him. He left school with hardly any academic qualifications and worked in menial types of jobs, then due to his indolent attitude he was not even accepted to do those. The final blow came when his mother died and he found he no longer had a roof over his head. He'd been dossing with friends in Liverpool and some kind neighbour had informed the local council that he spent weeks at a time away from his mother's home. Consequently, the council informed him that, as he was not a permanent member of the household, he could not take over the tenancy and would have to vacate the property.

From then on, his decline was swift. Eventually, he was sleeping rough. It was a terrifying existence, not knowing from day to day where his next meal was coming from, or indeed where he would be sleeping each night. Also, he was being constantly harassed, not only by the general public but also by those who were in the same position as himself. He had been beaten up. His few personal possessions had been stolen. He had been urinated on, and on one terrifying occasion awoke to find someone had poured petrol over him and set it alight. But for the close proximity of a water fountain, he could have died. Then there were the ones who sought to use him sexually. He resisted this until one particularly bleak rainy night he relented, out of sheer cold and hunger, and accompanied an old gentleman back to his house. He gorged himself on hot food and luxuriated in having a bath and a bed with clean sheets, but he had to recompense the old fellow for providing these "luxuries" in a way which was not to his liking. He vowed never to repeat that means of obtaining food and shelter ever again.

Begging was the way he had to survive and even that was fraught with a degree of potential danger, especially if you unknowingly occupied someone else's "patch". On several occasions, Stewart had been threatened and had even been confronted by one character who had drawn a knife on him for taking "his" place. On some locations it was possible, on a good day, to take more money than the statutory basic wage, but Stewart felt the loss of personal dignity and respect was totally crushing. Consequently, when he estimated that he had enough to see him through that particular day, he stopped and retired to the nearest café.

Stewart met one particular beggar named Charles (he never did get to know his surname) who always appeared with his down-at-heel shoes neatly polished and who always wore a tie, albeit a ragged one. He spoke with a refined accent. Charles spent many a happy hour with Stewart, sharing not only his alcohol but also his endless stories of his past life, which had included journeying to almost every part of the world, always in first class transportation and luxury hotel accommodation. The one thing he would never divulge was the reason he was now in his present predicament. One of the best pieces of information he gave Stewart was how to obtain food from supermarket waste disposal bins, which were situated at the rear of their premises. Some supermarkets locked their bins while others did not, and sometimes good-natured staff would leave tins and packets nearby. Charles showed Stewart the best places to go to obtain this bounty. This food was beyond its sell-by date but was still safe to eat. It was a true godsend to Stewart as it reduced the amount of time he had to spend begging. In consequence of this, and in a spirit of reciprocity, Stewart shared some of his best begging sites with Charles. Sadly, some months later, Charles committed suicide by throwing himself into the river.

Summer was the best time if you intended to sleep rough, if you could call living in such dire straits in anyway fortuitous. The accrued benefits of summer were warmth and more daylight, hence less likelihood of being attacked. Also, sunlit days tend to make people feel better and therefore more amenable to parting with their cash. But all too soon winter rolled around and the same old problems surfaced once again, only with the passage of each year there seemed to be more and more young people fighting for fewer and fewer places to rest their heads each night. Younger, stronger bodies would push you off your routine favourite begging spot, which in turn

43

pushed you even further down the contaminated greasy pole.

One especially inclement night, Stewart's only place to rest his weary bones was on a park bench. He was just about to settle down when it started to rain. Stewart noticed, as he prepared to recline, that the dustbin placed beside the bench had an umbrella sticking out of it. He quickly got hold of it and unfurled it. This action soon revealed why it had been discarded in the first place - it had two broken spokes. Nevertheless, Stewart proceeded to hold it aloft, as a little bit of protection was better than none. As he did so, a small piece of paper fell from within its opened material and fluttered to the ground. Stewart immediately recognized it as a lottery ticket and picked it up. This was not such an unusual occurrence as you might think, as Stewart had quite often found them scattered around the city. He always took them to the shop to have them checked, just in case a miracle might happen. On two occasions it had indeed worked out in his favour and had netted him ten pounds on each ticket. Although ninety-nine-point-nine percent of the time these trips to the shops were a waste, as time was the only commodity Stewart had plenty of, he did not mind doing it. It helped fill his otherwise boring day and there was always the tantalizing prospect that he might obtain a few pounds, though this was yet another indication of just how empty and small his life had become.

The sour-faced lady behind the shop counter looked at Stewart in her usual disdainful way as he proffered the ticket to her. She took it between her forefinger and thumb, as if what was being offered could give her leprosy. She entered it into the machine and waited for the results to appear. Mrs. Sour Puss continued to stare at the machine, and then annoyingly removed the ticket saying, "Damn machine, that can't be right." She put the ticket back in. Stewart saw her jaw drop and her face go ashen. Then, she turned to Stewart and said, "You have won, Sir."

Stewart knew that it must be a substantial amount, not only by the changed appearance of the woman's face but by her calling him "Sir" She started to call out loudly to everyone within earshot, "He's won a fortune."

"How much is it?" Stewart shouted.

But she just kept saying, "He's won a fortune."

"Give me my ticket, right now," Stewart shouted, more loudly.

Finally, she retrieved the ticket and handed it to him. Saying, "You've won six million pounds, six million."

By this time, a small group had gathered around Stewart, eager to be near him. A short while ago, they had pretended he was invisible. Now, with the mystic attraction of wealth, they pressed in on him, no doubt the superstitious among them hoping that his good luck would somehow be transposed to them. Stewart pushed his way past them and, clutching his prized possession, headed for the door.

It was still raining hard as he made his happy way along the empty path. His thinking and emotions had gone into overdrive. He started to fantasise about all the things he could do with such a vast amount of money - a new house, several cars, endless holidays, endless travelling, and a nice dog. He had always wanted a dog. A Jack Russell would suit him just fine. These thoughts and many other considered and silly potential purchases flooded his mind. Although the rain was now coming down like stair rods, he was totally oblivious to it as he floating along on a soft cushion of exalted blissfulness. Just at that precise moment, 85 year old Gideon Algernon Fairclough stepped unsteadily from the pavement onto the road, just as the number 33 bus was coming along, and due to the heavy rainfall, the driver did not see the old fellow until he was almost upon him. The driver turned the steering swiftly to the left and stepped on the brakes hard. The bus slewed to one side, narrowly missing old Fairclough, but due to the amount of rain, the bus aquaplaned and mounted the pavement. It struck Stewart hard, propelling him into the air, which sent him crashing into a brick wall. The violence of the impact was such that it broke both his arms and smashed in his skull.

Stewart's last vision in this world was to see his ticket fall from his inoperable hand onto the soaking wet pavement. It slid on its watery surface towards the gutter and continued its journey towards the storm grating, where it disappeared down into the sewer system. Even as Stewart's eyes closed in death, the symbolism of what had happened to the ticket and his life was not lost on him.

6. The Odyssey of a Misbegotten Soul

Reginald arrived at London's Euston station, early one weekday morning.

As soon as he had placed his feet on the station platform, a kind gentleman immediately offered to assist him with his luggage. Reginald attempted to resist, but his new friend was equally adamant in his desire to help. Not wanting to offend, Reginald acquiesced. The gentleman was such an athletic fellow that he quickly out-paced Reginald and ran directly into a large group of travellers. That was the last he saw of his luggage, which incidentally contained almost everything he owned, including his wallet.

Now somewhat shocked and on the verge of destitution, he attempted to gather his shattered thoughts. How was he to survive in the metropolis without money or a clean pair of underpants? As a boy, he had been advised always to have on clean underwear, in case he got run over by a bus and had to suffer the embarrassment of nurses seeing him in his undergarments.

He made his way towards what he thought was the exit. But after walking for some time, he realized he was in the underground system. Somewhat demoralised, he slumped down in the passageway, totally overcome with the oppressive heat and claustrophobic atmosphere of the place. He removed his jacket and hat and buried his head in his hands in despair and desperation.

Then he heard the distinct sound of coins being thrown into his cap. He looked up and saw a man in

47

the process of adding to the small mound of coins. "Have a good breakfast, mate," said the man, with a wink, and threw several one pound coins into Reginald's upturned hat.

Reginald's first reaction to this unwarranted kindness was to feel acute mortification that he was obviously being treated as some kind of vagabond. He quickly rose to regain his *amour proper* and lest some other philanthropic person feel obliged to thrust more money upon him.

Just as he was just about to stride off haughtily, he realized that, due to the kind misunderstanding general public who had taken pity on him, he was no longer in penury. He quickly counted out the money that had been gifted to him and found that it amounted to three pounds ninety-one pence - not an inconsiderable amount, considering that he had done absolutely nothing to warrant it.

He then made a quick calculation. If he remained at that same spot for, say, an hour, the money he would accrue would amount to about a pound a minute, which would be sixty pounds an hour. And if he spent five hours ensconced there, he could easily walk away with three hundred pounds - which would equate to what some city lawyers were being paid.

It seemed that London streets were indeed paved with gold - that is if you were willing to sublimate your self-esteem. But Reginald knew full well that it was not only beggars who had to put up with humiliating circumstances to attempt to make ends meet but also a great many supposed middle-class people who, while at work, tolerated terrible working conditions. It was probably some of these same people who had contributed towards the money he was now holding, as they empathized with the position in which they thought he was.

Food Glorious Food

Reginald speedily rejected any thought of begging to get by and, with regained fortitude and resolve, headed towards a branch of "Hunger Burger". It was the first time he had ever set foot in such an establishment. The tables and chairs were spartan in the extreme, with no table linen, and were bereft of any cutlery, place mats or even napkins. The whole place looked drab and austere.

He joined a queue which was headed towards a long counter, behind which stood several spotty unsmiling youths wearing silly little square hats and who were constantly running back and forth serving customers. The whole atmosphere was one of hurried, noisy food consumption. It strongly reminded Reginald of feeding time at the zoo. He soon reached the head of the queue and was confronted by an acne-faced teenager who sported a yellow badge, which indicated that he was the manager. He mouthed something incomprehensible to Reginald, who asked the youth to repeat what he had just said. The manager rattled off the same unintelligible words and waited for a response. The only part of the sentence Reginald could make out was, "Do you want flies with that?"

Thinking that he had yet again misheard, Reginald asked the youth to repeat the question. The now exasperated server pointed to coloured illustrations of

49

food displayed above the counter, each one marked with a number, doubtless to assist those customers who could not read or for foreigners and initiates like Reginald. He looked up at the highly inviting pictures of burgers and selected number three, which looked particularly appetising, with a sumptuous portion of nicely cooked beef topped with thick mouth watering cheese intermixed with fresh-looking lettuce.

He expressed his choice to the manager, who repeated the same phrase he had used earlier, "Do you want flies with that?"

Reginald remembered watching a TV programme about an African tribe who supplemented their meagre diet by cooking flies, which the presenter, Richard Attenborough, asserted were a source of high protein and therefore good for you. Whether the flies were edible and beneficial did not attract Reginald to consider ordering them, so he politely refused the server's inducement. Once the polystyrene-covered food arrived, the server plied Reginald with yet another unusual request.

"What do you think?" he asked.

"About what?" Reginald replied.

The youth cast his eyes upward and again pointed exasperatingly to a sign showing a happy-looking girl, un-ladylike, drinking from a brightly coloured bottle. The request now fully understood, Reginald nodded his approval of that particular beverage, which was speedily served to him already opened. He took hold of it and looked at the server once more. "And a glass, please," he said. The server did not bother to reply but looked towards the highly frustrated customer beside Reginald and said, "Next."

Reginald sat down beside the street-facing windows. The chairs were unsteady and uncomfortable - possibly, he thought, so that the customer would not spend too long sitting there after consuming their meal. He was famished and was looking forward to savouring his delicious burger.

This state of anticipation evaporated once he opened the carton to reveal the less-than-appetizing sight of a small, rather thin roll with an equally thin-looking filling of overcooked minced beef covered with odd-coloured plastic-looking cheese topped with a few wisps of limp lettuce. He brought the concoction up to his nose and sniffed it. Out the corner of his eye, he could see a customer looking at him quizzically. The burger smelt of fatty oil and nothing else.

Reginald was loath to put it into his mouth but he had no alternative as he was once again penniless, so shutting his eyes, he took a bite - and immediately wished he hadn't. It had the consistency of cardboard, with as much taste. The congealed contents shattered his taste buds with its cloggy mixture of monosodium glutamate and saturated fat. Reginald immediately christened it "The funeral director's friend".

Once Reginald had force-fed himself with the "burger" and consumed as little of the highly sugared drink as he could muster, he had a strong desire to clean his teeth, as he had that awful sticky objectionable feeling permeating every corner of his mouth. There was nothing he could do about it, as his toothbrush had been pilfered along with every other thing he'd owned.

He eased himself off the plastic chair and took another look at the pictures of the mouth-watering burgers advertised above the serving counter and thought that "Hunger Burger" should be prosecuted under the Trades Description Act. The young customer who had been watching Reginald's antics as he consumed his meal continued to do so and, as Reginald passed him by he said to him, "Bon appetite".

New Employment

Once out in the fresh air and feeling the first rumblings of indigestion, Reginald headed for a nearby park to contemplate his next move. He found a quiet spot with an empty bench and resignedly sat down.

It did not take long to assess his plight or what he could do to remedy the situation. He had no financial means of support, no accommodation, and no prospect of being employed, as he had no resident address. He therefore would have to swallow his pride and have a go at begging - or, to give it its archaic title, "To seek alms". That is, until he could generate enough cash to enable him to dig himself out of the financial hole he was in. Obviously, he would be required to sleep rough for the first few days. Then, hopefully, he could find suitable "squat" accommodation. He had heard prior to coming to London that there were many large empty houses, which were routinely used by squatters.

Reginald looked at the bench he was sitting on and the surrounding park and decided that this location would do him nicely as a temporary night abode. He made his way back to the station and headed for the same place he had occupied earlier and sat down. No sooner had he done this than someone stopped in front of him. Initially, Reginald thought it was a benefactor, but this idea was swiftly removed from his mind when he got a hard kick on his foot.

On looking up, he saw a very unkempt individual staring down at him and, before he could do or say anything, he was roughly grabbed by his arm and dragged to his feet. The smelly tramp pushed his unwashed face close to Reginald and, breathing Vodka fumes all over him, said, "This is my spot, so get your backside off it right now."

After the initial shock, Reginald quickly recovered. He was now on the horns of a dilemma. On the one hand, this could turn out to be quite nasty, both in physical injury and the distinct possibility that the police might become involved. But he also knew that, if he backed down now, word would undoubtedly circulate within the begging fraternity that he was a pushover, which could lead to him being attacked on a regular basis.

Reginald decided that his best line of resistance was to portray himself as being mad. Within most people, he knew, was an innate fear of those who behave strangely. He now put that theory into practice by pushing the tramp away from him and jumping up and down, simultaneously screaming at the top of his voice, "You're the devil, you're the devil, but you can't touch me." As he said this, he smiled inanely and stared wide-eyed at the tramp, who now backed away from him. Reginald quickly took advantage of this opportunity and rushed forward at the man, who now took to his heels and fled towards the escalator.

The battle won, Reginald reoccupied his rightful place and within half an hour had accumulated enough cash to pay for a light lunch, plus enough money for some items which he deemed necessary for his new position in life.

And so to Work

Reginald was a methodical person, so he approached his money-raising strategy in his usual way. He knew that, in his present attire, he did not convey the right image of a down-and-out. Therefore, he would have to alter his appearance. First, he made his way to a nearby charity shop to acquire a suitable jacket and headgear for his intended new employment. Once in the shop, he rummaged through several jackets, but was unable to find one decrepit enough looking for his purpose.

He was about to give up his search when a young lady approached him and asked if she could help. Reginald replied that she could and that he was looking for an old medium-sized jacket, preferably of dark colour. The fabric could be quite worn and faded, as it was for a play his church group were putting on. As an after-thought he asked, "And do you also have an old battered hat?"

All of these items were quickly acquired from the rejection pile of clothes at the rear of the shop and were placed in a large plastic bag. As he was about to leave, he spied a wooden walking stick and added that little prop to his wardrobe. Now, all Reginald had to do from time to time was perform a superman change of clothes routine by entering a telephone box as a neatly dressed man and exiting as a tramp. A good distance before Reginald arrived at the station to assume his rightful begging spot, he slipped into an alleyway and changed into his working clothes. He put his normal attire into the plastic bag and hobbled slowly into the station.

On arriving at his preordained alms-gathering position, he was surprised to see that it was already taken by another gentleman of the road. Reginald gave him short shrift by advancing on him with staring eyes and bared teeth, brandishing his newly acquired walking stick. He hoped, as he did so, that the beggar he'd confronted earlier in the day would have informed the local begging fraternity that there was now a madman operating amongst them and to give him a wide berth. This theory was soon substantiated when the beggar abandoned his stance and took to his heels.

Reginald sat down and placed his old hat beside his leg so he could keep a close eye on it. As he did so, he noticed a small cardboard box containing quite a few coins. Undoubtedly, they had belonged to the previous tenant, and as Reginald was now the new lord of this particular manor, he claimed rightful possession of them.

He counted out the coins, the value of which came to three pounds thirty-two pence, which Reginald thought was not a bad start to his working day. Reginald did not feel guilty in doing this, as he knew the previous owner was unlikely to return for them.

He was somewhat amazed at how swiftly he had assimilated the laws and operating procedures of the urban jungle, no doubt due to his introduction to penury and the threat of physical violence. So far, it had been only Reginald's superior intellect which had saved him from total defeat.

Reginald now started the grim and humiliating task of begging. As he had not yet attained a suitably unshaven look, he thought it expedient to keep his head down, which would also help in him not to see the people who were giving him money, somewhat lessening his feeling of mortification. The traffic through the passageway fluctuated in accordance with the arriving and departing trains. The first coin Reginald received was a fifty pence piece, which he quickly picked up and put in his pocket, as he intended never to spend it but keep it as a constant reminder of this terrible, humiliating period of his life.

As the day progressed, so did his income. Most people tended to give at least fifty pence, some even two or three pounds. Reginald thought about this for some time and he came to the conclusion that there were three reasons why some gave more liberally than others. Some were genuinely sorry for him. Or they could be trying to indicate, even to a down-and-out like him, that by giving him money they were acting magnanimously, which would indicate that they were in a superior social position. Alternatively, it could be for the giver's companion's benefit, to indicate how charitable the giver was. Reginald stopped trying to analyse the situation and settled on his first assumption that most of what he received was genuine charity given with honest intent.

By lunchtime, Reginald was feeling quite hungry so he decided to retreat to the nearest café. This, of course, would require yet another change of clothes, so he went to the station toilets and did his quick-change dress act once again. He chose the nearest cheap and not quite cheerful quick food joint and settled down to his ubiquitous burger, hoping that this time it would be better. However, it tasted as bad as it looked. But it was sustenance and that was all he was looking for in his present predicament.

He had chosen to pay the higher sit-down price (VAT included) for his meal, as this gave him the ability to use the toilet facilities and the opportunity to rest his weary bones. He looked about him and at the other customers. Almost without exception, none appeared to be happy or enjoying what they were eating. So, in some senses, anyone looking at him and any of the other customers would be hard-put to spot any difference in their respective social standing. This was the type of thought and observation that would have never occurred to Reginald but for the position he now occupied.

Once he had eaten, but not been refreshed or satisfied, Reginald headed back to his "patch". On the way there, he saw another beggar, only this one had a dog sitting beside him. Reginald watched him for a few moments and noted that a substantial number of people gave something to the young beggar, far above what Reginald had received. This could only be because of the dog's presence, as there are approximately eight million dog owners in Britain and, in all probability, double that figure who liked dogs. Reginald could see the financial necessity of acquiring a dog as a "prop" to help boost his potential income.

As Reginald approached his begging station, he saw that it was occupied by yet another usurper. Reginald decided to use the same frightening technique he had used before. He rushed at the unsuspecting man with his walking stick held high in the air, screaming at the top of his voice. As Reginald was six feet three, he must have made quite a sight as he headed for the intruder, who made a hasty exit, leaving Reginald to settle himself down in the Lotus position once again and wait for alms to cascade into his capacious hat, all the while hoping that it would be a copious amount so that his sojourn on the ground would not be long.

The hours ticked by. Business was slow, with only the intermittent sound of coins dropping into the fedora. Once six o'clock had arrived and the rush hour was well and truly over, it was not worth remaining there any longer. It was time to tally up the day's takings. It did not take him long, as he found that the total receipts came to five pounds and sixty-one pence. Clearly, he had miscalculated his potential earnings. At this rate, it would be some considerable time before he could replace everything that had been stolen from him.

He toyed with the idea of packing it all in and hitching a lift back to his home town - something he had vowed he would never do when had originally set out for London. Now, however, he could clearly see that begging did not seem to be the answer to his temporary predicament - that is, unless he could find a way of increasing his takings.

Once more, he made his way to the burger joint to challenge his digestive system with another episode of gastronomic Russian roulette. This time, he tried something called the "Big Fry". Once again, it bore no relation to the succulent picture depicted on the advertising display above the service counter. Reginald sent up a silent prayer as he bit into it, imploring the good Lord to strengthen his digestive tract, as he was about to abuse it severely. He quickly consumed the disgusting food and attempted to wash the cloggy taste of saturated fat from his mouth by drinking something which purported to be orange juice. However, the only thing that was orange about it was the orange-coloured picture on its label. He resolved never to visit that particular establishment again.

Accommodation

Reginald was a good cook and he knew that he could eat much better and cheaper by preparing his own meals. The only problem was finding a suitable "squat" somewhere nearby. With that in mind, he set off, scouring the near-by side roads. An hour later, he'd found one. It was a very large Victorian structure with an imposing frontage, albeit in dire need of substantial repair. But it was more than suitable for him and was certainly a massive improvement to sleeping on a park bench. He circumnavigated it, looking for a weak spot in the surrounding high fence, but could see none. Systematically, he pushed at each individual wooden fence slat until two of them moved aside, which was just wide enough to allow him to squeeze through into the back garden. It was then quite easy to gain entry, as one of the boarded up windows was ajar. Reginald felt euphoric at his accomplishment and mockingly said aloud, "I lay claim to this house."

Reginald sat down on one of the few remaining chairs and surveyed his new tenancy. Casting his eye around the room, he could just imagine what it was like in its heyday. The room had lovely proportions, being approximately thirty-five feet by twenty with a fifteen feet high ceiling, richly decorated in fine plasterwork. He could just visualize a ball being held there in Victorian times. Ladies with crinoline dresses, men in military uniforms and others in tail coats, dancing the night away, unaware that in the future the British empire would be no more and the house would be vacant and derelict.

At this point in his ruminations, Reginald was rudely interrupted. He suddenly heard loud sounds coming from the upstairs area, which clearly indicated that he was not alone in the property.

He quickly made his way towards the stairs and rushed up, as the sounds were increasing in both volume and pitch. Reginald could now clearly distinguish that it was the voice of a woman, and a woman who was obviously in some distress.

Once he reached the upper area, the sounds of the woman's voice continued unabated. It was difficult to tell which room the sound was coming from, due to it reverberating around the large empty spaces. Finally, he arrived at the correct one and was confronted by the sight of a man and woman struggling on the floor.

By the half undressed appearance of the woman and her continual screaming it was obvious that he had interrupted a potential rape attempt. The man was powerfully built with long hair and an unkempt appearance. They were so engrossed that they were as yet unaware of Reginald's arrival. This state of affairs was soon altered when Reginald struck the potential rapist a solid blow to the head, which propelled him some distance across the room. Both the man and the woman looked astonished at Reginald, who in turn now wondered what was about to happen next.

The man shook his head and stood up revealing that he was almost as tall as Reginald, only he looked a good five stone heavier. He had a nasty looking face with a deep scar running diagonally across his right cheek - not the type of person one would like to meet in a dark alley - or in an old Victorian derelict house.

"Who the hell are you?" said the man-mountain.

Reginald tried to swallow but his throat was too dry.

"What's the difference who I am," he managed to rasp out, "the question is what do you think you were doing to the woman?"

"Whatever I was doing is none of your bloody business," Scarface retorted, "and if you don't get out of here right now I'll do a lot worse to you!"

With that informative pronouncement, the man moved towards Reginald, who stepped backward until a broken chair impeded his retreat. Grasping it to balance himself and trying to look unperturbed by the threat, he attempted to stand his decidedly shaky ground. The man then made a headlong rush at Reginald, who deftly stepped aside, and the man collided with the chair and collapsed in a heap on the floor. Reginald stood with his fists clenched ready for the retaliation that was sure to fallow. None came. Scarface lay prostrate on the ground, moaning deeply. Reginald waited for some time before going over as he thought that he might be feigning injury. This was allayed when the man said that he was sure he had broken some of his ribs. Reginald bent closer to him and gingerly turned him over, at which the man gave out a loud shout of pain. The woman said, "Serves you right, you brute!" At the same time she raised her stiletto heal to injure her assailant even further, but Reginald grabbed her foot and said, "Enough, now let's get him out of here." The woman resignedly agreed. The old adage came to his mind "Hell hath no fury like a woman's scorn".

The main reason Reginald wanted to get the man out of the house and into the garden before calling an ambulance was to make sure that the ambulance crew didn't report that the house was being occupied. Moving such a large man was no mean task and one in which the woman refused to assist. Reginald initially thought this mean spirited, until he got a better look at her very bruised and battered face, which clearly showed that she had undergone a considerable beating. After witnessing the extent of the woman's injuries, he wasn't too bothered about how much pain the man was in and so was less careful about how he handled him from the room towards the stairway. The only assistance the woman provided was to clear a pathway along the landing until they reached the stairs. Getting the man down the stairs presented them with a new problem. Reginald thought about it for a few moments, while all the while the man continued to groan in pain and the woman continued to smile.

"Have you got any ideas for getting this man down the stairs?" he said to the woman.

"How about kicking him down!"

Reginald ignored her and looked around for something on which to lay Scarface, who by now was looking none too good. The only thing he could find which might help was a *chaise longue* which fortunately had wheels. He wheeled it over to the head of the stairs, upturned it then picked up a large brass candlestick and proceeded to batter the legs off. He then went over to the high bay window to remove the thick curtain ropes, which he secured to one end of the *chaise longue*. He struggled to get the injured man on it and had to use more rope to secure the brute firmly in place. With the belated help of the woman they gradually lowered the *chaise longue* downward, step-by-step, which took a long time. When it had almost reached the bottom of the stairs, the woman let the rope slip through her hand and Reginald was unable to stop the couch careering swiftly to the floor which sent its passenger smashing onto the marble floor. His screams of pain could be heard reverberating throughout the house. Reginald looked at the woman who looked back at him coyly and saying, "Oh I'm ever so sorry, I just couldn't hold it," she smiled sweetly and moved off.

Once they had untied the man from the *chaise longue*, Reginald set about opening the large oak front door, using the same heavy candlestick to smash away the lock. They dragged and pushed the dead weight of the man into the garden. Reginald could see that the woman was enjoying this, as each time they moved the man, he gave out screams of pain. Eventually the Herculean task was complete. Reginald then went over to the front garden fence and kicked several pieces of the fence slats out to allow the medics to get the injured man to the ambulance. He told the woman to hide in the house while he went to call the ambulance, but she replied, "You don't need to do that – I've got a mobile phone."

He made the call then bent down to instruct Mr. Scarface to tell the medics that he had been injured in the garden and not to mention that anyone else was here. Otherwise, he would let the police know that he had witnessed him beating and trying to rape the woman. The state of her face and his supportive testimony would clearly prove that this was true, so that it was in his own best interests to agree. Scarface readily acquiesced.

Reginald and the woman retreated to the house, closing the door just in case the police might want to check it. The ambulance arrived within ten minutes and swiftly removed the man, but fortunately the police were not in attendance. Once they had departed, Reginald made good the fence opening and very firmly secured the front door. They waited anxiously for an hour, until it seemed safe that Scarface had not revealed that they were in the house.

Now that the hubbub had died down, Reginald looked more closely at the woman. She appeared to be about thirty five years of age with natural blond hair and a good figure, but was not exactly one of nature's beauties. The bruises that the brute had inflicted on her were starting to discolour her skin, particularly under her left eye. Reginald felt sorry for her and was just about to introduce himself when she suddenly said, "Thank you so very much for what you did for me - I truly thought he was going to kill me."

"Think nothing of it," he replied. "How long did you know him?"

"I didn't, I just turned around and there he was. He grabbed me and said 'I won't hurt you as long as you don't scream,' which was exactly what I did, so he started to beat me until you intervened."

"Which I was more than happy to do," Reginald said and stuck out his hand. "By the way, I'm Reginald."

"And I'm Senga," she replied smiling.

As he clasped her small hand in his, she flinched.

"My hand is still very sore from trying to beat that brute off."

Reginald gave her a sympathetic smile and said, "Do you think you need medical help?"

"No, no. I've lived through much worse than this, I'll be fine once I have a rest."

Senga showed Reginald to the very large kitchen, where she had cleared a small area for preparing hot food and drink. She had a small paraffin heater to heat water and cook on. She also had a collection of mismatched kitchen utensils, all obtained from charity shops. All in all it was quite a nice little set up. Senga offered to make coffee, but he insisted that she rest and he would make it. They sat down and got to know each other a bit better. Senga had arrived at the house several months ago and, at that time, there was another young couple living there but they had moved out and since then she had felt quite vulnerable in such a large and isolated mansion.

"I suppose it was your intension to live here when you entered this house?" Senga said.

"Yes it was, and still is, that is if you have no objections?"

"Not in the least, after what you did for me." Senga smiled, adding, "Have you brought anything with you, sleeping bag etc?"

"Only the clothes I stand up in, as all my worldly possessions were stolen from me the moment I set foot in London."

She gave him an understanding smile and said, "The same happened to me, only it took three days to have mine pilfered - I was very naive when I first arrived here."

He thought, and so was I, but he kept that embarrassing truth to himself.

Reginald wandered around the mansion looking for a room to move into, particularly one which had not been too vandalized. He found what he was looking for in the attic; it was small and rather cramped, possibly a servant's room in days gone by. It had a small skylight window, which gave a wonderful view of the city. He wondered what poor unfortunate servant had occupied this room. He could visualize the poor devil having to get up very early each morning to tend to the needs of the rich family and, in the winter, get up even earlier to light the numerous coal fires scattered throughout the house.

Needless to say, there were no fires in the servants' quarters and they had to sleep covered only with thin bed sheets. He remembered reading that a lot of the female staff in these big houses used to sleep in the same bed just to keep warm. Some of the male servants did the same but for quite different reasons.

In the days that followed, Reginald explored the rest of the mansion and was delighted to find that the water supply had been turned off only at the internal valve in the basement. Slowly, by trial and error, he was able to find out where the many water leaks were. He sealed them and got a supply flowing to the kitchen and the downstairs bathroom. He then salvaged a toilet from the second floor bathroom and reconnected it downstairs. They now had running water and a working toilet, the very essence of civilized living.

Gracious Living

Reginald and Senga had settled into a regular routine, each having breakfast at eight then leaving for 'Work' at eight thirty. Neither of them ever asked what the other one did during the day, but both contributed their fair share to the weekly budget. Anyone taking an objective view would have assumed that Reginald and Senga were a couple, and if they could have observed them of an evening, this assumption would have been reinforced in seeing them sitting by the fireside reading and conversing like an old married couple. Senga even planted vegetables in the garden. At no time did either of them broach the question of why they were now in this situation.

Reginald's original estimation of potential earnings from begging was far from being realized, so he started to research the reason why. He took some time off from his strenuous duties to have a walk around and observe other beggars' modus operandi, and he soon observed that those with a dog took considerably much more money. The dog obviously pulled at the heartstrings and generosity of the giver more than the plight of the beggar. Reginald resolved to obtain a suitable placid dog, but the question was how? Also, would Senga be happy to have a dog in the house? At dinner that same night Reginald tentatively put the question to Senga and her reaction was just what he had anticipated.

"A dog! Why would we need a dog?"

Reginald was not keen on telling her the real reason, so he replied, "Well it would be good for our protection."

Senga was quick to point out the downside asking, "And who would be looking after it during the day while we are out, and who I might ask would be cleaning up its poo? I for one would not."

"I would be quite happy to do that."

"And what if it starts barking when we're not here? What then, I'll tell you what - people would be calling the RSPCA, who would break into the house and then where would we be?"

Then, sounding like Maggie Thatcher she concluded, "The answer is no, no, no."

With that pronouncement, she disappeared behind her newspaper, clearly indicating that the matter had now been settled. However, the matter would be resolved in Reginald's favour in the not too distant future, in a way he couldn't possibly have foreseen.

Serendipity

Reginald's coffers always accumulated substantially whenever there was a football match on. He always bought two cheap supporters shirts - one for the home team and one for the visitors. As the police didn't allow the two teams supporters to travel on the same train, it was a golden opportunity to make a substantial financial killing. He got to know which team's train was due at the station and would put on the shirt of that team, taking care not to get the time table mixed up. With his hat prominently in front of him (bearing a ribbon of the team colours), Reginald sat there suitably attired looking the very picture of a fellow supporter down on his luck. The money rained into his hat, so much so that he intermittently had to empty it into a large bag. There were always other events taking place in the capital - Art, Sport, Exhibitions etc, all of which helped Reginald milk money from the travellers as they journeyed to and from these events. He was doing very well, but always in the back of his mind was how much better he could be doing if only he had the added attraction of a dog beside him.

He had watched a few dogs pass by as he sat in his usual spot every day. Most had been assisting blind people. Of the others, he had assumed that their owners were nearby, until one day a dog lay down beside him and remained with him throughout the day. Needless to say, Reginald's income increased substantially. He shared his lunch with it. Although he didn't know much about dogs, this one looked like a Jack Russell, and was mostly white, with a spotted black face. It was very cute and friendly, which was a big asset in Reginald's type of work. The nametag on its collar revealed it was called "Bingo", but there was no address. The dog sat placidly by Reginald's side all day then suddenly at three thirty it got up and started to walk towards the station platform. He followed it as quickly as he could, all the time calling out its name, which the dog completely ignored. On reaching the platform, the dog stopped and, when the three thirty five train arrived and all the passengers boarded, he quickly jumped on board just as the doors were closing.

Reginald stood there dumfounded, not only by the dog's unusual behaviour, but more importantly by his loss of an excellent fundraising partner. Before the train moved off, he looked in at the dog for the last time, or so he thought. As he was about to walk away, the Stationmaster came over to him.

"I could see you were concerned about Bingo, well don't be, he'll be back tomorrow on the ten thirty. He has been doing that for the past three years. At first we tried to stop him, but we couldn't, so we learned to leave him to his own devices. He's a clean little fellow and we now look upon him as the station mascot."

With that the Stationmaster departed, leaving behind a somewhat startled, but much-relieved Reginald.

Reginald spent a restless night, turning and tossing

in bed wondering and hoping what the Stationmaster had said was true. Next morning, he made his anxious way to the station and waited on the platform for the ten thirty to arrive. He felt a bit stupid standing there waiting for a dog to arrive on time, probably, he thought, the Stationmaster was hiding somewhere looking at him and having a good laugh at his expense. Nevertheless, he decided to tough it out and wait to see if his little business partner would report for work.

The ten thirty was late, which only increased the tension. When it arrived, the doors flew open and the hoards poured from it with no sign of Bingo. Reginald felt extremely silly as he walked away, but he had only gone a few yards when he suddenly felt the pressure of a dog brush against his leg. Bingo was looking up at him, wagging his tail. Reginald picked him up to hug him.

The weeks seemed to fly past. Reginald's original intention of only begging long enough to get back on his feet and find a well paid job began to falter when he enquired what those 'well paid' jobs were paying? He started to change his mind and rationalize his situation - what was the point of giving up this nice little earner to go and work for less money and most certainly less freedom?

That didn't make much sense to him as he was clearing, on average, three hundred and fifty pounds per week and only having to 'work' five hours a day. He would be crazy to give it up before he had accrued a nice nest egg, tax free of course, plus he was living in a rent free mansion.

Shotgun Persuasion

Throughout his tenancy there were intermittent attempts by individuals to enter the mansion and evict Reginald and Senga, but all of them were unsuccessful, as Reginald was always one step ahead of them. The worst of these was when a group of men had managed to get as far as the hallway, only to be confronted by Reginald pointing a shotgun at them. He had found an old twelve bore deep in the basement and thought that the sheer sight of a gun would be enough to scare the living daylights out of them, but he was wrong as they steadily advanced towards him. Reginald shouted at them to stop or he would shoot, and to show the seriousness of his intent he cocked the gun.

"Bluff as much as you want mate," the leader of the gang said, "but we are taking over this house right, as we have plans for it now, and you and your little lady friend should scarper while you have the chance."

Reginald backed up as they advanced, until he tripped on the edge of an old rug. The gun went off with a thunderous noise and blew a large hole in one of the windows. The explosive sound reverberated around the hall and the interlopers took to their heels and swiftly departed. The blast also scared the living daylights out of Reginald and Senga, as they had always assumed it was not loaded. However, the incident had a positive benefit, as the potential usurpers told every other vagrant not to go near the old mansion, because it was occupied by a total nutter, who was quite willing to shoot them.

The warm summer days soon merged into the colder days of autumn, which also had a bearing on the generosity of people. This didn't concern Reginald much, as he was still taking enough money each day to stay afloat and have enough left over to add to the stash of money hidden under the bedroom floorboards. He also bought a solitary lottery ticket each week. Initially, he religiously checked the numbers in the vain hope of winning, but as time went by, he purchased them more out of habit than of expectation. Then, out of the blue it happened, his numbers came up - he had won not millions, but a very welcome ten thousand pounds. He bought a good quality radio, two paraffin lamps and other items to make their life as comfortable as possible. It suddenly struck him that acquiring these small comforts was in a way tacit admission that he intended to go on living in this house and continue begging for some time to come.

Now that the chilly nights were with them, the need to keep warm in such a large damp house soon became apparent. The only thing Reginald could do, as his tiny attic room had no fireplace, was to heap more blankets on the bed and even that did not fully keep out the cold when the temperatures plummeted. Senga, on the other hand, had quite a large fireplace in her expansive room, which she kept supplied with timber from the overgrown garden. She felt a bit guilty that she was in a much more comfortable room than Reginald and that, but for his intervention, she might have been killed. So she suggested that it would be a better idea if he moved in with her on a temporary basis and he could sleep on the large *chaise longue*. Reginald didn't resist this helpful suggestion and moved most of his belongings down into Senga's warm room. They also decided to have their meals in her room, as it was larger and, more importantly, had that very necessary fireplace. Reginald bought a large extending dining table from a charity shop and placed it directly in front of the fireplace. It vastly improved the look of the room, particularly when having their evening meal - it took on a new and highly pleasing atmosphere with its blazing fire and soft candlelight.

Things went along like this for some time, during which they got to know each other a lot better. Neither of them was willing to fully confess why they were in London in the first place, or indeed reveal anything about their background. They were different in so many ways, yet so alike in the fundamentals of what constitutes friendship. In essence, they got on extremely well with each other, probably better than a lot of married couples. The only part of their relationship missing was sex. Although Reginald found Senga attractive and good fun to be with, he could never envisage being in love with her, which was exactly how Senga felt about him. Both had been celibate since living in London, not only because they hadn't met anyone they desired, but also because of the physical and emotional tension of trying to survive in the rural jungle that was London. Now however, as a lot of their frustrations and deprivations had been removed, their natural sex drive started to reassert itself. This become evident during a particularly bitter cold night, when Reginald had forgotten to bring in enough firewood. By the time he realized his oversight, it was snowing very hard, so he resorted to breaking up the only wood that was available to him, namely what was left of the old *chaise longue*. Soon however, it too was consumed and, in the wee small hours, they both could feel the bitter cold night air permeate their bedclothes.

After some time Senga whispered to Reginald, "Are you awake Reg?"

"How could I possibly not be in this damned cold!" he tartly replied.

She ignored his rudeness and said, "I was just thinking, would it not be better if we shared the same bed - that way we could cuddle up together to keep warm - what do you say?"

"I'd cuddle up to a polar bear right now if it kept me warm," Reginald replied with the same frosty attitude.

"Don't be cheeky and get yourself over here right now."

Once he was in, Senga said, "Now I don't want any hanky panky from you while we're in the same bed, so I'll sleep on one side of the sheet and you on the other side, ok?"

Reginald, who was still frozen, was more than happy to agree. Sex was the last thing on his mind at that icy moment, however once they had snuggled together and began to warm up, things started to alter for both of the sex deprived bedfellows.

Although Reginald's natural sexuality was being inflamed by being in such close proximity to Senga, nevertheless he tried to curtail his natural instinct and was to a degree managing to do so, that was until Senga moved herself very close to him. He could feel the warmth and softness of her body through the bed sheet and this proved just too much of a temptation and he quickly moved over to the same side as her and waited for her response, she didn't object.

He fully embraced the now equally inflamed Senga. Neither of them said a word as they touched each other intimately for the first time. Reginald had almost forgotten the supreme emotional and physical pleasure that could be derived by being held in a woman's arms, to feel the silky smoothness of her skin on his and the ultimate joy of sexual union. Looking at Senga objectively, no one would have thought someone who looked so unprepossessing could possibly arouse such high passion. Although they both had different personal agendas and, in no way could their association be described as love, nevertheless they had now attained a level of satisfaction and mutual trust which more than satisfied each of their personal needs. From that point on, to all intents and purposes they lived as if they were a married couple, yet still retained the freedom to keep certain personal information strictly private. They had found a satisfactory equilibrium within the confines of that old mansion.

Reginald now reviewed his situation. He had, by this time, accrued quite a bit of money, more than enough to stop begging and start looking for a decent job. He had rent-free accommodation and a decent sex life, so it was now time to implement the reason why he had initially set out for London. He could not involve Senga in this decision, as that would mean telling her what he had been doing for a living, which was not something which he wanted to do. Plus, he had no idea what she did. He started to make enquiries at the job centre and found to his dismay that there was very few jobs available, with the exception of those that paid only the statuary basic wage which was far less than he could accrue begging. He would also be required to work ten hours a day with a starting time of eight thirty! Nevertheless, he thought he would give it a try, so after the usual formalities he was given an address of a fast food joint in the periphery of the city centre. His interview was succinct and to the point. The first question he was asked was, "Do you speak English?" Then it was, "Let me see your hands" and finally, "Any breakages will come out of your wages." He passed all these arduous requirements with flying colours and was thrown an apron, silly hat and a pair of rubber gloves before being unceremoniously ushered out of the office of the "Manager", who looked about sixteen years of age. Reginald's new working life had begun.

Getting up at the ungodly hour of seven thirty took a good deal of will power. After having a quick breakfast and serving Senga's in bed, he headed for work. The smell that normally pervades fast food outlets is bad enough during the day, but smelling these establishments once they have remained closed all night is something not to be recommended. His first task was to sweep, scrape and wash the previous day's crusty morsels and grease from the floor, then do the same on the tables and chairs, swiftly followed by cleaning the toilets. When he had finished these uplifting tasks, he came to the conclusion that this type of work could not be considered a step up from what he had been doing during the past months - he found it to be just as demeaning and a lot less profitable. Nevertheless, he stuck it out and within the week had graduated to be a server. His only training was to always ask the customer, "Do you want fries with that?" Almost all of the customers were teenagers whose knowledge of proper food could be easily written on the back of a postage stamp. Initially, Reginald thought that the customers frequented the place only because they were poor, but this proved not to be the case when he observed the expensive motorcycles and fancy cars they owned.

Senga did not always arrive back 'home' at the same time each day, Reginald never asked her why, primarily as that would have lead onto other associated questions, so when they sat down for dinner was something of a moving feast. One night, as Reginald decided to pick up some specialised cheese from a little shop, which took him from his routine way home. He suddenly saw Senga on the other side of the road with the same old battered oblong case that usually sat beside the doorway in her room. He was going to shout across to her but decided not to, as she was so engrossed with the old case. Due to the volume of traffic he was unable to get to her and, as he watched, he saw her pull from the case something that looked like two pieces of wood. She placed the case on the ground then started to screw the two wooden objects together.

By this time Reginald was both enthralled and more than a bit bemused. He wondered what she would do next, but did not have long to wait as she suddenly put the joined pieces to her mouth and blew. The sound was terrific and highly musical; the pieces of wood were obviously a clarinet. Reginald was astonished watching her playing and also observing people throwing money into her wooden case. It suddenly became clear, Senga was a Busker and that's why she didn't reveal what she did for a living. This newly acquired information made him speculate on why she came to London in the first place, as she had obviously been professionally trained. Now more than ever, he wanted to know the answer to that question, but he had no intention of asking her, Her secret would remain so, that is of course unless she volunteered to reveal it, which he hoped in due time, she would.

During Reginald's second week at the gastronomes' nightmare, he discovered that the place was employing illegal immigrants and paying them only two pounds an hour. This enraged him, as he knew that the place was doing extremely well and could easily afford to pay much more than that. He knew that there was very little he could do, as it was a 'Catch 22' situation. If anyone reported what was going on, there was a strong possibility that the illegals would be deported, plus the business would be fined thousands of pounds and might close altogether, thus making all of the workers unemployed, including himself.

As well as the very young Manager, there was also a much older supervisor who relished his little bit of power and tended to find fault in almost everyone, especially the illegal immigrants. He heaped humiliation on them, as he knew that there was no way they could retaliate. He foolishly thought he could treat Reginald in the same way, but this was his undoing and he was about to meet his Waterloo. It all came about one afternoon when Reginald let a bottle of ketchup sauce fall, and a good amount splashed over the supervisor's shoes. His response to this was to castigate Reginald in front of a lot of customers by calling him everything but a gentleman and shouting at him to get down on his knees and clean it up.

"And what have I to clean it up with?" Reginald said to him.

"With this you stupid git," the supervisor retorted, throwing a rag in Reginald's face.

"Oh I don't think that will be big enough to do the job," Reginald said, "I think I'll have to use something a bit bigger."

And with that he pushed the supervisor to the floor and dragged him back and forth over the spilt ketchup, much to the amusement and loud applause of the staff and customers. Thus ended Reginald's sojourn into the catering trade. He returned once more to the happy land of the mendicant.

Birthdays Come but Once a Year

Reginald was getting more and more emotionally attached to Senga and, now that he was aware of what she did each day, he wanted to know more about her prior to their meeting. However, he was keenly aware that she wanted to keep her previous life private and he didn't want to pressure her in any way, as he was in a similar position.

He thought the best method was to slowly and surreptitiously extract it from her. He had no idea what age she was, not that it really mattered to him, but she was a bit of a conundrum, in that he usually found it pretty easy to guess a person's age, give or take a year or two, but with Senga he was totally stumped. Her face could best be described as acceptable more than pretty and there was nothing in it to indicate her age.

So Reginald set himself the task of finding out Senga's age and it took him a little while to come up with a plan with a fair chance of achieving its objective. As he was now aware that she was a musician, he purchased a CD player for her along with several classical CDs and a birthday card. He presented them to her saying, "Happy birthday!" She was totally surprised by this and blurted out "But my birthday isn't until the 5th of July!"

"Then you can be like the Queen who has two birthdays - the official one and her actual one - so this is your official gift and you'll have another one on the 5th of July."

Senga smiled broadly and opened the birthday card and read it.

"You cheeky old devil - I'm only thirty one, not forty!"

Snap, he had succeeded. He had deliberately bought that card knowing that it would in all probability be the wrong age. He feigned surprise and said, "Oh I'm sorry, I didn't notice it had an age printed on it." That CD player gave both of them hours of pleasure and satisfaction. It was truly wonderful sitting close together in the candlelit room next to the blazing wood fire listening to wonderful music. In the future, Reginald intended to elicit further information from Senga, but only if she not be aware of. He wanted to know as much as possible about her, as she was now very important to him in so many ways. He didn't want this to be a one-way street, as he also intended to reveal to her his own past life, in a similar intermittent fashion.

Bingo

Once Reginald had re-established himself back on his old patch - after having to evict the temporary resident - he also re-established his relationship with Bingo.

He had missed the little dog more than he could have ever imagined and felt a bit guilty in abandoning it, however Bingo did not hold this against him and treated Reginald in his usual rumbustious and tail wagging way. The dog meant more to him than merely an attraction to get money from sympathizing patrons. It totally mystified Reginald and the station staff how the dog knew what station to get off at each time. Reginald thought perhaps the dog had a kind of internal clock to estimate the journey time, but he dismissed this as fanciful nonsense. He studied Bingo getting off the train over a few days and noticed he always stood for a few moments sniffing the air before alighting. Reginald's theory was that, as a dog's sense of smell is hundreds of times better than a human's, Bingo was using that same acute ability to recognize the correct station. Each station smelt different to the dog, so it could quite easily tell when it was time to get off.

Reginald was equally fascinated to know where the dog went each time it left him at the end of the day. He decided to find out the only way he could by simply getting on the same train as Bingo. Bingo was not in the least perturbed by Reginald's unusual action of travelling with him on the train but happily sat beside him until they reached Angel station. There it made its exit and lopped along the station platform with Reginald in hot pursuit. On leaving the station, Bingo headed north, which soon took them towards the shopping area then onward to a neat collection of Victorian houses. Bingo looked back at Reginald and, seeing him struggle and slow down, the dog also cut its speed to allow him to catch up. They proceeded for a few hundred yards further then Bingo bounded up the driveway towards a substantial white painted house and was immediately greeted by a small girl who cradled him in her arms and said, "Where do you get to each day, you silly dog?" Reginald had seen enough to both satisfy his curiosity and his concern that Bingo had a good home.

A New Tenant

Reginald always bought a lottery ticket each week, but never the Euro draw, as he considered the odds were even more stacked against winning. He restricted himself to purchasing only one, which was as much as he was willing to gamble. It added a little bit vivacity to each week in that, if they won, in one fell swoop they could transport themselves to a new style of unabashed living. Reginald did from time to time win, but only very small amounts, then one day he hit the jackpot. It wasn't a great amount - £5,000 - but large enough to extract them from their present penury. Reginald didn't immediately tell Senga of this good fortune, as he planned to do so that very night and booked a table at a local restaurant for the occasion. Meanwhile, he placed the ticket in his money hide-a-way box under the floorboards and left for his last day of begging, primarily to say goodbye to Bingo. Once at the station, he didn't bother to occupy his usual stance but walked around the tunnels with Bingo. Finally it was time to say a fond farewell to his little companion and, as he bent down to touch him for the last time, at that precise moment a rat scuttled past. Needless to say Bingo went in for the kill and ran after it with Reginald taking up the rear.

The pursuit took them to the station platform, where the trio ran between the assembled passengers. The rat, due to its small size was more nimble than Bingo, especially when turning. It suddenly made a swift turn at the edge of the platform. Poor little Bingo tried desperately to apply the brakes by digging his claws into the smooth stonework, but was unable to stop and skidded over the platform edge, landing on the track, thankfully not making contact with the power rail. Reginald pushed his way through the peering passengers and was aghast at the sight of little Bingo frozen with fright at being down in an area where he had always been protected from entering. The dog was in extreme danger and all he had to do to be killed was to move a few inches to

84

bring him into contact with the live rail! Reginald didn't hesitate, but quickly lowered himself down to where Bingo was, all the while being advised by travellers not to be so stupid and to leave the dog where it was. This was the last thing Reginald would have done. He approached Bingo very slowly and said to him, "Stay Bingo, stay." The dog obeyed him and stood rock steady while Reginald scooped him up in his arms and pushed him onto the platform much to the delight of the cheering travellers. This was the last sound Reginald was to hear, as the nine thirty two train emerged from the tunnel and sliced into him. He died instantly. Once his body had been removed and taken to the mortuary, the morticians could not find any forms of ID on him, so they attached a label to his big toe that merely read "Unidentified".

Back at the mansion, Senga was busy preparing the evening meal - a pizza with fresh tomato and rocket salad - Reginald's favourite food. He was normally home on the dot of five. Senga was not initially concerned when he didn't arrive on time, but as time progressed, she became more and more anxious. Much later, she knew something had happened to him and became frantic, as she had no idea where he went to once he left the house each day. Also, she didn't know his surname just as he didn't know hers. So how could she go to the police and request that they search for someone when there was so little information to go on? She couldn't show them any photographs of him or ask them to contact his relatives; she had simply nothing to offer them for any potential search. She continued to stay at the mansion for a month, always hoping that a miracle might happen and that Reginald would come walking through the door. Of course he never would and finally Senga resigned herself to that fact and tearfully left the mansion for the last time.

Sometime later, as the drip, drip sound of water could be heard splashing onto a cooking pot left in the kitchen sink in the old mansion, a strong hand grasped the tap and turned it until the dripping stopped. A new resident had just arrived and had taken possession of the house. Yet another chapter was about to begin in the long history of that old Victorian mansion.

7. The Black Dog

Tom had a sharp analytical inventive mind and he was constantly engaged in perfecting solutions in every aspect of his life. The particular problem he was in the process of solving at the moment he had thought about for some considerable time. Gradually its solution began to become apparent. He had worked out all possible parameters such as the minimum drop to achieve the required outcome, the tensile strength of the suspension cordage, now it was time to move beyond theory and start towards the desired end of his long delayed plan. Tom was a perfectionist and he would not agree to going ahead with anything until he was totally satisfied that it was as near perfect as he could make it, this attitude was in some circumstances commendable while in others it could be considered an obstruction to getting things done expeditiously.

It was this same pernickety attitude which led to the downfall of Tom's marriage, he always demanded that his wife work to a strict preordained timetable set out by him, this ranged from what time they arose, to the exact time their meals were to be served, even how the table napkins were to be folded. His poor wife put up with this for many more years then she should have, then suddenly one Sunday she took what money was available and fled in the middle of the night, never to be seen again, leaving a note for Tom which simply read, "Departed 3.30 AM sharp, won't be coming back, hope not to see you again in this life, or the next. Without love, Nicola."

Tom had inherited a very viable business from his

astute father who had been a wily business man who had balanced the cost of production against the margins of making the product with acceptable quality at an attractive price which in turn kept their factory ticking along nicely, consequently keeping the family coffers filled. That was until Tom took over the helm after his father's death. He immediately instituted 'Improvements' into almost everything they made, which of course had the effect of increasing the price of production, the cost of which was passed on to its customers which inevitably lead to a very sharp decline in demand, eventually leading to its closure.

Now solely reliant on what savings his father had accrued Tom persisted in his obdurate attitude in everything he did, he had kept this side of his character under wraps while his father was alive, but now without that restraining hand, he ran amok, spending money as if there was no tomorrow, in consequence of which within a short while he was penniless and in the end had to sell the family home just to pay off his debts.

Churchill called it his "Black Dog", Winston's name for the all-encompassing blackness of depression. This was what now encapsulated Tom within its suffocating folds. Now without the company of people or proper food or shelter, he slid ever deeper and deeper into the depths of melancholy. Tom eventually found a place by the river which gave him a semblance of shelter, it was an abandoned warehouse within which was situated a wooden hut which he had rigged up as a bedroom complete with a dirty mattress and pillow, once he shut its door each night he felt more secure, the only thing that bothered him was a large rat, which from time to time paid him an unwanted visit, Tom had tried to kill it by every means possible, by trap, poison and even chasing it with an iron bar, none of these worked. The rat had possibly been a resident long before Tom had decided to establish himself there. This fellow inhabitant only added to Tom's depression, and moved him further down the black despondent tunnel of despair.

Tom awoke one cold rainy winter morning and felt chilled to the bone, he already had a touch of arthritis and as he exercised his numb fingers they started to pain him even more as the blood started to circulate within them. Tom slipped into a deep cloud of mental blackness, which prompted him to bring into operation the plan he had so long harboured.

Calmly and slowly he left the hut and walked over to a flight of steps, climbed them to the first level to where a rope hung down from one of the steel girders which Tom had placed there some time ago in preparation for what he was now about to do, he placed the noose around his neck and without further delay launched himself into eternity.

Tom had read that people who attempt to kill themselves often report that their entire life flashes before them. This did not happen to Tom. From the instant he dropped off the staircase the only thing that flashed threw his brain was that he did not want to die, but now too late he plunged to his inevitable death. During each millisecond he was in screaming agony, this was quickly cut short as the rope snapped taut with a resounding whip-cracking sound.

89

Tom's eyes opened to a world of pain, not only from the deeply embedded rope burn around his neck but also the pulsating agony from every part of his body which had come into crushing contact with the concrete floor. Gasping for breath he tore the rope from his neck and gulped air into his heaving lungs.

After a while he sat up marvelling that he was still alive. He continued to sit there for some time trying to regain some normality to both mind and body, and eventually he found enough strength to drag himself to his hut for a very welcome swig of whisky.

Now somewhat fortified, Tom made his unsteady way back to the steps to solve the conundrum of why he had managed to survive the suicide attempt. Although he was overwhelmed with delight to still be alive, he was however mystified as to the reason why the rope had failed, as he had tested it to well beyond its breaking strain. Anyone else would have been ecstatic with relief and joy at still being alive and left it at that, but not Tom. Even with such a close brush with death, Tom's exacting nature still demanded that he seek out the precise reason why the rope had not supported his weight. It was only when he inspected it closely that he noticed a series of teeth marks at the point where it had failed, Tom readily recognized that they had been made by the rodent that frequented the building and had often taken bites out of other things owned by him. Tom laughed aloud at this revelation and thought that he must be the only man in history whose life had been saved by a rat.

What had happened in that dingy building totally transformed Tom, gone was his depressive gloomy outlook on life and was replaced by the revelation how truly wonderful being alive could be. Sometimes it is only when we are about to lose something does its importance and worth shine through and we come to recognize its true value, sadly for a lot of people that realization comes too late.

8. Rescued from P45

The sound of garbage trucks trundling along the street and the constant racket of the wheelie bins being emptied woke Malcolm. This routine commotion signalled that it was Monday. Now that he was unemployed, each day seemed like any other and they all morphed into one continuous, boring, never-ending treadmill. When he had been working, each day had a different feeling - no two days were alike and the weekend in particular was the time he really lived. Friday was expectation day, that slightly tingling sensation that the weekend was almost upon him with all its exciting possibilities. Malcolm never planned anything, he just let the weekend happen. He liked a drink, but never got drunk. He observed that those who did drink to excess soon found out what the booze could do to you once it was in control. He loved the company of women - all shapes, all sizes - in particular the older birds who were always grateful for what they got. They didn't expect you to get too serious and they well knew that the chances of him staying were slim, so the time they spent together was all the more exciting and intense.

Malcolm didn't bother with chat up lines when trying to pick up a girl, he used his tried and tested, simple technique of just looking at a girl, not staring, but just a gentle look of fascination. Nine times out of ten this would be reciprocated, through her body language, how she might toss her hair, or give that slight sideways glance in his direction. He in turn would then look directly into her eyes and, if she didn't look away, he knew that the bait had been taken. Everyone wants to be desired, loved and appreciated, be that women or men, young or old, single or married, ugly or beautiful. This was the key Malcolm used to open the box of delights each exciting weekend, or at least, that's how it used to be. Now that he was unemployed and skint, such delights were a thing of the past as he had no dosh for taxis, booze or entrance fees to clubs. He felt castrated, metaphorically and physically. Malcolm had a simple, yet philosophical view on life, namely as we all have a sell by date of about 75 years, why waste any of it doing things we don't like rather than trying to experience as many exciting things as possible. The only fly in the ointment of that theory was that we have to eat and need creature comforts; hence, unfortunately, the necessity of having a job.

Like most things in life, it is only when we actually experience something personally that we realize how it truly feels, be that something joyous or sad, both of which moves you beyond merely sympathizing with someone's plight, but gives a you much deeper ability to empathize with them. Before becoming unemployed, Malcolm used to think that the out-of-work were, on the whole, just a bunch of lazy scroungers who were quite happy to let the state provide for them (he had been a tabloid reader), but now that he was experiencing the brutal reality of unemployment, his attitude had undergone a total transformation. He had met quite a few fellow jobseekers who had made applications for hundreds of jobs, yet were still unemployed and now he was climbing that same bitter league of the disenchanted.

The only bright lights on his jobless horizon were

the fortuitous and intermittent associations with some of his past sexual conquests. He was more than happy when this happened, as he found the state of being celibate was not at all to his liking. He craved not only the climatic act of sexual union, but also the sheer joy of being in female company. He loved the sight, feel and touch of a woman and only felt truly alive when he was in intimate association with them. He pleasured in making women happy, not just physically, but also creating an aura of happiness in their day-to-day life. He treated each one like a queen, whether they were pretty or not. During these transient meetings, he was often aware that a good number of his married conquests often lived very dull, pedestrian and unhappy lives - each day making breakfast, packed lunches for the kids and the boring husband whom, when they were first married, behaved like Casanova, but very quickly degenerated into the hunchback of Notre Dame. Her only free and happy moments were snatched when she was in the house on her own doing the never-ending, mind-numbing chores of making beds, washing, dusting, preparing meals etc.

Some of these women, when taking a coffee break from this soul-destroying work would fondly caress the silver bracelet they habitually wore, which would immediately take their minds back to the exciting liaisons with Malcolm. These little bracelets had been a job lot Malcolm purchased from a friend in the jewellery business who had sold them off at a knockdown price. They were high quality, heavy 925 sterling silver. Initially Malcolm had bought them to resell, but changed his mind when he saw how happy it made the first girl he gave one to and thereafter he presented one to each girl he made love to. He had lost count of how many were being worn in his local community - let's just say he quite often saw one on display as he made his way around town from week to week. Malcolm always adhered to his primary philosophy that life was not a rehearsal to prepare us for something better - we only have one crack at it, so should attempt to enjoy each and every day, share as much happiness as possible and build up a store of precious memories.

Paramour

One particular recipient of a silver bracelet was a girl called Victoria, a charming and very sensual married woman who Malcolm met when he was employed at the local electronics factory. Needless to say, when she showed an interest in Malcolm he was keen to present her with a bracelet. She wore it only three days after their first meeting. He was totally infatuated with her - she fulfilled almost everything he physically desired in a woman, as well as being very bright with a good sense of humour, not a combination too readily found, in his experience. He adored her and, had she been single, he would have married her at the drop of a hat. There was however one flaw in her make-up - she believed that you should never get divorced, even if you recognized that you were with the wrong partner. He had tried to disabuse her of this silly idea, but to no avail. It was the only stupid thing Malcolm had ever heard her utter. Then one day when they met at their usual rendezvous, he saw that she had a nasty swollen eye and a cut on her lovely lip. When Malcolm asked how she came by these injuries, she attempted to lie by saying she fell while in the garden. He quickly reminded her that she had told him previously that they did not have a garden, as they lived in a high rise flat, and he asked her to tell him the truth. Tearfully, Victoria told him that there had been an argument with her husband over money and his excessive drinking. One word had followed another and he had hit her. Malcolm was incensed and immediately said he would sort the coward out, but Victoria pleaded with him not to do anything as she was sure he would never do anything like that again. Purely to please her, Malcolm reluctantly agreed.

Needless to say, three weeks later she once again turned up with more injuries, this time a cut above her right eye, which she tried to hide from Malcolm. He was enraged when he saw it and once again Victoria made strenuous efforts to calm him down. Malcolm could see that his anger was upsetting her, so he lied and said, "All right Victoria, don't get upset but make sure this is the last time anything like this happens to you."

In truth Malcolm had already made up his mind that her cowardly husband would pay, and pay dearly, for what he had done to that lovely girl and he set about organizing a time and place for retribution.

Over the following week Malcolm prepared to mete out justifiable revenge on Victoria's husband. First, he surreptitiously gained as much information from Victoria about him and his daily routine as he could without raising her suspicions. Malcolm reconnoitred his victim's journey to and from the pub he frequented. He always used the same short cut to the back door of the hostelry, only this time it would be a short cut to severe pain. Malcolm concluded that the best time to mount the attack was just after he left the "Drake & Duck". There was an area of poorly lit scrub ground, which was ideal.

All of this planning and stalking might seem like some sort of military manoeuvre, which to a degree it was, as Malcolm had served fifteen years in the army. He had seen action in Iraq and Afghanistan, where he witnessed some truly dreadful things, including his mates being blown up by roadside bombs and others losing arms and legs, so seeing that a drunken sod got what was coming to him didn't bother Malcolm in the slightest. He bought a black ski mask and a baseball bat, both second-hand, so they couldn't be traced back to him. He was now more than ready to dish out some long overdue corrective punishment.

On the appointed night, Malcolm waited for an hour in the darkness of some trees close by the scrub land and, right on time for his appointment with pain, the substantial portly frame of Victoria's husband staggered out. It was obvious that he had, as usual, imbibed more booze than was good for him and was now making his unsteady way across the open ground towards his fate. Malcolm was about to make it a night the wife-beater would never forget.

He pulled the ski mask down over his face. Initially, he had planned to come stealthily up behind his victim, but changed his mind because he wanted the brute to fearfully see what was about to happen. Malcolm stepped out from the bushes and swung the baseball bat high in the air. When the drunk saw this, he tried to turn and flee, but Malcolm caught him a solid blow behind the right knee. He buckled and folded like a penknife, and fell on his back. Malcolm had an immediate flashback to Afghanistan, where he had carried out similar individual attacks on Taliban insurgents. It had been brutal and decidedly very personal, especially when you were close enough to your victim to smell his sweat and feel the convulsions when you knifed him to death. As a consequence of performing such deeds, Malcolm had suffered from post-traumatic stress syndrome (PTSS) and it had taken him a long time to recover. What he was now doing seemed to reignite his previous illness. He was on automatic and, ignoring the cries for mercy, he brought the club down hard onto his victim's fat stomach, then directed his next blow directly onto his testicles. Any man who has been unfortunate enough to have suffered even a slight injury in that hyper-sensitive area will tell you that it is one of the most excruciating pains you can inflict, shattering every nerve ending in the groin area. The trauma was so great that the man's vocal cords were immobilised with shock, but this was not the end of his travail. Malcolm now stepped on the victim's right wrist, which made the man involuntarily open his hand wide, and Malcolm brought the club down unsparingly onto the thumb, pulverising the whole bone structure, so that the thumb would have to be amputated. This brutal method was often used in Afghanistan to make sure that suspected Taliban fighters would, in the future, be unable to handle a gun. Luckily for Victoria's husband, Malcolm suddenly came to his senses and stopped the attack. He looked down at his victim to assess the damage and was shocked by what he saw. Looking around to see if he had been observed, he bent down and removed the man's wallet, then made his escape towards the river area where he threw the wallet into the water, purely as a ruse to make the police think that the attack had been perpetrated by a mugger.

When Victoria told Malcolm about the mugging how her husband would have to stay in hospital for some time due to the beating and also to have his thumb amputated, Malcolm feigned surprise but said that this was just what the brute deserved. During her husbands stay in hospital, they saw each other as much as possible and on his release, Victoria told Malcolm that he had changed in that he was fearful of going out at night, which reduced his alcohol intake and that he had stopped beating her.

"Well something good came out of that beating he received," Malcolm said adding, "if I knew who that mugger was I'd shake his hand."

As he said this, he clasped his hands together behind his back in self-congratulation. The police did find one piece of evidence, namely the baseball bat that Malcolm had thrown into a wheelie bin. He had done this deliberately to create as much frustration for the police as possible and so that they would waste a lot time and effort trying to find out where it had been purchased and sending it to their forensic department for analysis. However, he had worn gloves and there were no fingerprints on it. With no other evidence or witnesses, the police, just as he had predicted, lost interest in the case and buried it in the their ever expanding "Unsolved crime" archive files, tabulated under "Random mugging" and it was very soon forgotten. Everything had worked precisely to Malcolm's plan. Although the revenge attack had worked out successfully it had thrown up a new problem for Malcolm in that he had found that his PTSS had not been totally healed. It apparently still lay dormant just beneath a thin layer of social normality.

A Visit From The Dark Angel

Things remained on an even keel for some time, but then Malcolm became aware that Victoria was becoming more and more unhappy each time they came together. On pressing her for a reason, she said that her husband had once again had started to abuse her, only this time the brute chose to do so by means of mental torture, which can often be more damaging than being physically assaulted. Malcolm was at a loss of what to do other than advise her, as he had done previously, to divorce him, something she still refused to contemplate. It was a constant worry to Malcolm and he even thought of paying her husband another 'social' visit, but was fearful that he might not be able to contain himself this time and remove her tormentor permanently.

One day, right out of the blue, Victoria phoned Malcolm to say that she could no longer suffer the daily mental anguish and humiliation, and had decided to divorce her husband. Malcolm was euphoric with pleasure and arranged to meet her in town in an hour. As he paced up and down outside a little Italian restaurant they frequented, he suddenly saw her across the street waving frantically at him and looking more like her usual beautiful self. Malcolm thought that this moment was the most wonderful of his life and waited impatiently for her to arrive. He watched as she suddenly rushed out between two vehicles and one ploughed straight into her! He stood there for a moment unable to accept what he had just witnessed then rushed, just as heedless of the traffic, over to where she lay. A small group had already gathered around her and one person was giving her CPR. Malcolm pushed his way through the throng and knelt beside Victoria, who showed no signs of movement. He attempted to get closer but was rebuffed by a man administering to her, who roughly pushed Malcolm aside saying he was a doctor. The doctor turned to the crowd and shouted out, "Has anyone called for an ambulance?" A few replied, "Yes."

Malcolm had never been a believer in prayer, but at that moment he ceaselessly sent up prayers of intersession on her behalf. Finally, an ambulance arrived and Victoria was gently lifted into it. Before the crew closed the doors, Malcolm rushed forward and told the medics he was her husband. They quickly ushered him into the vehicle and with sirens screaming headed for the hospital.

He watched anxiously as the doctor worked on Victoria. Thankfully the hospital was not too far from the scene of the accident and once there Victoria was speedily propelled into the operating theatre. Malcolm was totally distraught waiting to hear how badly she was injured and all the while he prayed frantically for her. Within a short time, the door of the room was opened and a doctor, still dressed in his operating clothes, stepped into the room. His face conveyed what Malcolm had been dreading to hear. The doctor spoke for some time but the only words Malcolm heard were the last ones, when he put his hand on Malcolm's shoulder and said, "I'm so very sorry, we could not save her."

Malcolm stumbled his way out of the hospital into the darkness of a London night, totally oblivious to the pouring rain, which mingled with his cascading tears. He walked for a long time and it was only the hypothermic cold that brought him to seek shelter in a café, where the heat and a large mug of coffee started to revive his circulation and mental equilibrium. He felt as if his heart had been physically ripped from his body and the tears flowed from him in a never-ending stream. Some customers looked at him strangely and a kind waitress asked if he was alright. Malcolm looked at her and thought, what a question, but managed to give her a slight smile in reply. The waitress suggested that he move over beside the radiator, which would help to dry his clothes. Malcolm nodded thank you and headed towards the heat, past a table with four tough looking teenagers sitting at it.

"Better do as your mummy tells you little boy," one of them said in a derogatory voice and the rest of the group laughed.

Malcolm stopped in his tracks and turned to look at them, his face suddenly transformed from that of a shattered and distraught man to one of murderous intent. His eyes took on a strange look as he moved forward and picked up a knife from the table. The usual hubbub of conversation and laughter in the cafe ceased abruptly and all eyes were now focused on Malcolm. The tension and silence in the cafe was almost tangible. A girl rose from a seat nearby, but a swift glance from Malcolm made her sit back down. It was now the turn of the young men to change their attitude from bullying boastfulness to cringing fear, and they grouped closely together like frightened children, pressing themselves against the wall.

A battle was going on in Malcolm's mind and emotions - he was trying to subdue the impulse to rain down violence on that immature little gang. Instead, he slowly placed the knife back on the table and moved over to where the waitress was. Within seconds, the boys had run out of the café ignoring the continuing downpour. Malcolm had secured another small victory over his PTSS.

The days that followed conveyed to Malcolm just how much he had loved Victoria and the time leading up to her funeral was passed in deep cutting mental pain and self-recriminating anguish. There were the usual newspaper obituary notices, which indicated where the service would be held, and the time and place of the interment. He had every intention of attending both.

He sold his watch and sent a large wreath with a note inscribed "From a friend who will miss your sweet presence each and every day". He would have liked to have clearly stated something far more personal but decided it was not the time to reveal what he and Victoria had meant to each other.

The night before the funeral Malcolm did not sleep at all, but spent the time going over and over in his mind how Victoria's death could have been avoided. The only paradoxical thought he could come up with was that, if he had never met her in the first place, she would still be alive. He was swimming in a sea of guilt, which only began to recede once daylight came. He made his way to church, something he hadn't done since he was a boy.

He had been educated at a Catholic school, but had avoided going to church as much as possible. He had quite forgotten how very ornate Catholic churches were with their ostentatious decor, statues and the abundance of pictures on the walls depicting episodes in the life and death of Christ, and with the all pervading sickly sweet smell of incense hanging heavily in the air. Victoria's coffin was placed right in front of the altar, the sight of which totally pulverised Malcolm's emotions.

There was quite a large turnout, with of course Victoria's brutish husband in attendance looking suitably sad, and other members of her immediate family. The service passed in a haze of words and genuflecting, then the coffin was borne out. Malcolm had managed to scrounge the taxi fare and arrived at the crematory at the same time as the cortege. The early morning drizzle had stopped, and the sun made a brief appearance and thankfully stayed throughout the protracted interment rites. As Malcolm watched the coffin being lowered into the grave, he felt as if he was also being buried.

Once Victoria had been laid to rest and the mourners had departed, Malcolm made his way to the graveside. He took a single red rose (which had been Victoria's favourite flower and colour) and placed it on her grave, then spent some time in contemplation during which his tears flowed freely. Malcolm had been so engrossed that he had failed to see a tall older gentleman observing him from a distance. This same man now made his way over to Malcolm, who was totally unaware of his presence, until he placed his hand on his arm.

"I hope you don't mind but I'd like to have a word with you." He offered his hand and said, "I am Victoria's uncle."

Malcolm shook his hand and the man continued, "My eye was drawn to you at the service and also here at Victoria's grave. By your gestures it is obvious that she meant a great deal to you - I used to be a policeman and old habits die hard."

"I was a work colleague and friend of Victoria - she was a truly lovely girl."

"That she was, that she most assuredly was," the old gentleman replied. "Why don't you come back with me to the house for a refreshment and meet the rest of the family, I'm sure they would be very happy to meet old friends of Victoria's and you could tell them about your relationship."

This of course was the very last thing that Malcolm wanted to do, plus the thought of being in close proximity to Victoria's husband was an anathema to him. He was just about to refuse the old gentleman's offer when it suddenly started to rain very hard, so they both sprinted to the shelter of the car, and once there Malcolm told the old fellow that he would rather go straight home.

Victoria's uncle agreed to take him home, as it looked as if it would be raining for some time, but he persisted in asking Malcolm to at least stop off at Victoria's house for a short while, then he would quite willingly run him back. Malcolm looked out at the pounding rain and thought, what the heck, I may as well go. Malcolm's decision was not flippant, but based on a desire to see where Victoria had lived a goodly part of her life.

Once at the house, Malcolm was introduced to Victoria's friends, and of course expressed his condolences to the bereaved family. Malcolm studiously tried to avoid meeting the grieving widower, but Victoria's uncle intervened and guided Malcolm over to meet the husband, whom of course Malcolm had met intimately on a previous and highly satisfying occasion. Malcolm was pleased to see that his handiwork had born fruit in that the brute had indeed lost his right thumb. The uncle introduced Malcolm, who took this opportunity to grasp the husband's hand in a vice-like grip shaking it as firmly as he possibly could, which resulted in a scream of pain. Malcolm feigned surprise, apologized for not noticing the injury and asked how it had happened. "Oh just an industrial accident," the brute lied. Malcolm felt a bit better as he walked away but felt compelled to go to the bathroom to wash his hand.

Victoria's uncle continued to guide Malcolm around the room until they came to a tall blonde woman who smiled broadly as she was introduced to him.

"I'll leave you two young people to get to know each other and go and see if Bob needs a hand," the uncle said, whoever Bob was.

The woman was called Elizabeth. Malcolm was uneasy in her presence and he was aware that she was scrutinizing him closely as if trying to assess him in some way. To break the stalemate, Malcolm said, "Have we met before?"

"No but I have a premonition about you."

"Well I hope it is a good one," Malcolm said jokingly.

"I think we had a connection through a very dear friend of mine," she replied unsmiling.

The use of the past tense indicated that she was referring to Victoria. Before Malcolm could respond, the woman continued by saying, "Yes I'm sure I'm right." Malcolm stared at her for a moment and thought, how on earth do women have such intuition?

"And what makes you think that?" he replied, knowing this sounded hollow and defensive.

"I'll tell you why, my dear Malcolm, because Victoria told me in the strictest confidence that she had met and fallen in love with someone else. She didn't tell me your name, but described you in detail, and as soon as I saw you, I knew that you were that person."

"I'm more than happy to say you are correct," Malcolm said with a guarded smile. "I'm sorry but could I have your name again, it's just that I'm not exactly myself right now."

"I understand perfectly Malcolm, I'm Elisabeth Drummond."

She put her hand on Malcolm's arm and suggested

107

that they continue their conversation in the privacy of the garden. They walked towards a little secluded arbour where they sat down. Over an hour, Elizabeth recounted the whole sordid truth of poor Victoria's existence with her brutish husband. She told him of many instances of harsh and brutal treatment, including Victoria being dragged by her hair across the room, being punched on a regular basis and, even when pregnant, being thrown down the stairs resulting in the loss of her baby. Malcolm had to ask Elizabeth to stop as he couldn't bear to hear any more.

"I'm sorry Malcolm, I was not thinking, it's just that I have been bottling this inside of me for such a long time."

"Victoria told me a little of what was going on but I never knew it was that bad."

On hearing this Elizabeth gave him that same quizzical look as when they were introduced.

"You of course knew that Victoria's husband was mugged recently and that he lost his thumb in the attack?" she said scrutinizing Malcolm's face intently.

"Yes, was that not awful?" he replied but couldn't contain a smile, which Elizabeth reciprocated.

"Now I wonder what nice man could have done such a nasty deed?"

Elizabeth said that many a time on hearing what Victoria put up with she could have cheerfully murdered the brute and Malcolm replied, "You'd have to stand in line."

They parted as firm friends. Elizabeth's farewell words were, "I was so delighted when Victoria told me about you, although I had more than an inkling someone decent had come into her life as she changed out of all recognition. That made me desperate to meet the man who was responsible for such a lovely transformation, and now that I have, I can well see why she fell in love with you."

Malcolm blushed as she kissed him goodbye.

The lifeline

Not long after Victoria's funeral, a letter arrived with an invitation to attend a job interview at a local factory called "Drummond Chemicals Ltd". The job on offer was for an assistant chief security guard. Malcolm had made so many job applications for all types of work over the past months that he couldn't remember if this had been one of them or not, nevertheless he duly made his way to the factory on the appointed day. He was directed to the main administration building, all ultra modern and hi-tech, and took the lift to the top floor where he entered a large reception area. A secretary told him to have a seat and that Mr. Drummond would see him shortly. As Malcolm sat there, he studied the signs on the wall depicting all the products Drummond chemicals made, then the name Drummond suddenly struck him - that was the same name of Victoria's friend who he had met at the funeral! Malcolm's first instinct was to leave, as he didn't want any preferential or charitable treatment, however wiser self-counselling prevailed and he stayed to see if his assumption was correct. There was only a short delay before he was shown into the Director's wood panelled office. Behind the inevitable large desk sat a moustachioed bald headed man, who smiled at Malcolm as he entered the room. The man rose and came over to Malcolm with outstretched hand.

"Welcome, I'm Tony Drummond, Director of the company."

After formal introductions, the Director motioned Malcolm to sit down and then selected a chair beside him. Malcolm appreciated the Director conducting the interview this way rather than from behind his large imposing desk.

"Now the reason I'm interviewing you," the Director said, "is quite simply that my wife was highly impressed on meeting you, so purely on her recommendations that is why you are here today. Now tell me about yourself, your work experience etc."

"Well I've had quite a few jobs since I left the army."

"Oh so you were in the army, what regiment?"

"I was a sergeant in the Logistics Corps, bomb disposal unit, served fifteen years and saw action in Iraq and Afghanistan. Unfortunately I was wounded by a roadside bomb and was invalided out with a foot injury, or I would still be serving today."

The Director smiled and nodded.

"I was also in the army, spent ten happy years in the Artillery, then stupidly resigned my commission to take charge of the company when the old man died, have always regretted it, but that's all water under the bridge now."

They spent an hour reminiscing about their days in the military, then the Director said, "Well Malcolm you'll be happy to know that I have decided to take you on. To be truthful, I was hoping to get someone with a military background and you seem to fit the bill exactly. There will of course be the usual trial period of a month and if you prove satisfactory, which no doubt you will be, you will be taken on in a permanent basis."

The Director shook hands with Malcolm and told him to see his secretary in the anteroom, where she would assist him in filling out the necessary paperwork. He would then be taken to the stores to be measured for his uniform, which he would pick up on the following Monday before starting work. On leaving the factory, Malcolm was euphoric at the prospect of once again working and earning a decent salary. However, his mood changed immediately when he thought how happy it would have made Victoria to share in this little moment of victory with him. He would have many more lonely and bleak times when he would feel like this and would tell you that the old adage that "Time heals all wounds" was a lie. He had found that we never fully recover from certain traumatic things in our lives, no matter how many years have elapsed - we just pretend that the pain no longer exists but in truth it is only dormant, and given the right circumstances it can once again come back to haunt us.

And so to Work

The following Monday, Malcolm was suited out in his uniform and it felt strange to once again being kitted out like a soldier. Unlike some of the other security uniforms Malcolm had seen, which made the wearer look like bit of a clown, this company's was restrained and dignified, so no doubt the Director had a hand in its design. Malcolm was given a large folder containing all the detailed instructions for his shift work. He was then accompanied by an older guard, who showed him what they were required to do on each shift. The work was certainly not onerous but was repetitive, if not downright boring, but Malcolm was happy to be at long last gainfully employed, which meant he could start to pay off his outstanding debts. In essence he was a happy man, with the exception of the periods when his mind drifted back to thinking about his lost love, Victoria.

There were six security guards, two groups of three working alternative shifts. Malcolm liked the occasional night shift, as it gave him time to catch up on his reading.

He devoured almost any kind of literature and his latest book was called "The subterranean recesses of the mind". It asserted that the mind operated on not two levels, but on three. The first being the conscious, the second the subconscious, the latter being the interconnecting system between those two which, under certain intensely stressful situations, could influence the conscious mind in ways alien to it and could compel it to perform deeds abhorrent to the rational mind.

As a sufferer of PTSS, Malcolm could well see the validity of this hypothesis. There would be many times during forthcoming workdays when this book would readily come to mind.

One day as he was making his rounds, Malcolm

got a massive surprise when someone called out to him and, on looking around, found Victoria's husband staring at him saying, "You must be the new guard."

Malcolm nodded. It was obvious that the brute didn't recognize that he had already met him at Victoria's funeral - possibly the uniform added to that misconception. Thankfully at that juncture Malcolm heard his name being called again and turned round to see the Director who said, "Just popped out for a bit of fresh air and you're just the man I was hoping to meet."

Then, seeing the brute also standing there he added, "I take it you have already been introduced to the foreman of our special section unit?"

Before Malcolm could reply the brute interjected, saying "No sir."

"Ah well," the Director said, pointing at the brute, "this is Dexter, who is a foreman in one of our special sections, and this is Malcolm our new assistant chief guard."

Malcolm was pleased that the Director had spoken his Christian name, but only used the brute's surname. The brute put out his hand and Malcolm had no option but to grasp it. It felt just as rough, sweaty and disgusting to hold as Dexter looked. At the first opportunity, he would find the nearest toilet and cleanse the foul DNA contamination from his hand.

The director looked at Malcolm and said, "I'd like a word with you," then looking over to Dexter he said "Thank you Dexter," who replied, "Sir", before turning on his heal and departing.

"The reason I wanted a private word with you is to ask you if you would be interested in taking up a vacant position in our special section?" the Director said.

"I had no idea there was a special section!" Malcolm replied.

The Director was quick to enlighten him. "The special section is a separate part within the factory complex, it deals with top secret and classified material, the exact function of which I'm not at liberty to divulge to you until you sign the Official Secrets Act, that is of course if you are willing to transfer. Now, are you interested?"

Without waiting for a reply he continued, "I should add that the post carries better conditions of service plus higher re-numeration and I'd like your answer right now Malcolm!"

Malcolm did not hesitate for a moment and said he would be delighted to transfer. The Director told Malcolm that he had checked him out against the Police National Computer and, other than a few parking tickets, he had passed the assessment with flying colours. The Director asked Malcolm to present himself at the Personnel Director's office on Monday morning for full assessment and to complete all the necessary paperwork.

The Director was just about to leave when Malcolm suddenly remembered about dear Dexter, and asked what authority he would have over the other employees within the special section. The Director's answer was swift and to the point.

"Total - security comes first and you will only answer to me."

That had been the answer that Malcolm had hoped to hear, as it left no room for any interference from the charming Dexter.

The following Monday, Malcolm duly went to the Personal Director's office and completed all of the necessary official forms. He was then taken on a tour of the special unit, accompanied by another guard. They entered a lift to descend to the special unit high security departments. Malcolm noted that as he entered the lift that the panel had ten buttons on it, yet from the outside of the building there appeared to be only three floors. The lift descended very quickly and smoothly until the tenth floor button was illuminated, indicating that they were now a considerable distance underground.

The tour of the units took the rest of the day, as it was a sprawling labyrinth of a place. Malcolm quipped to his companion that you would almost need a SatNav to find your way around it.

"You'll get used to it in a month or two and, by the way, have you noticed that each area we enter the staff wear different coloured uniforms? This is to make sure that they do not attempt to enter any other department," his fellow guard explained. "Each department is painted a different colour, which matches the uniform being worn in that particular department, so that if anyone was to enter the wrong department it would immediately be noticed by the CCTV monitoring staff. The only people who have total accesses to all units is senior management and security personnel."

The underground units even had their own medical departments, restaurants, power supply, high filtration air conditioning and, most importantly, a very sophisticated security system, which included 30 very high definition CCTV cameras. Each room could be automatically sealed from a central control room and gas could be pumped into any individual unit to overcome any intruders. In essence, it was a totally self contained, sealed community. The construction cost must have been astronomical.

Malcolm had to spend several days studying the substantial rules and procedures of working in the unit, particularly as it was a potential target for terrorists. He was then transported to a nearby army shooting range to test his shooting skills and, while there, was informed that he had a license to use maximum force on anyone trying to gain access to the special unit. Malcolm spent a further week being chaperoned by another guard before he was finally put in control of his own section.

Contrary to what he had originally thought, there was very little time for sitting around, as he had to constantly patrol each department within his section. This procedure required that he press a security button the moment he left the control room, which gave him a set time to reach the next station - now he could see why his medical examination had been so thorough. If he didn't arrive on time at the next station, the alarm would go off and all the units would automatically be sealed off. It certainly was the ideal job for anyone who wanted to keep fit. The duty hours were two on, one off, which was to make sure that the guards were always operating at maximum efficiency.

Weeks passed during which Malcolm gradually

got used to the awkward hours of working. Throughout all of this time, he didn't see the charming Dexter, which helped Malcolm to stabilize his emotional turmoil. Then suddenly he saw him or, at least, he saw a hand resting on a car windowsill as it drove past. The car passed so quickly that Malcolm didn't have an opportunity to see a face but he distinctly saw that the hand had a thumb missing! He could once again feel the long restrained anger exploded within him. Malcolm knew from past experience that the best method of keeping his PTSS at bay was to try to avoid coming into contact with Dexter, however fate would deem this not to be possible.

Should Auld Acquaintance be Forgot

One night, a call was received from the production factory asking if they could have the aid of two men to assist in getting a chemical storage feed motor restarted. As Malcolm was off duty, he volunteered to help and was told that another man would assist him. It wasn't until Malcolm got into the vehicle to take him over to the factory that he suddenly found he was sitting beside Dexter, who tried to make conversation. Malcolm was barely civil, as he still had a boiling hatred for the brute.

Once they had entered number four section of the factory, the manger described the technicalities and told them they would be required to climb the outside stairway to the top of the storage vessel. Hopefully they would be able to restart the air input motor, which pumped compressed air into the mixture and, if the motor had burnt out they would have to haul a new one up and fit it. He asked them if they felt competent to carry out the task and both affirmed that they were. It was only at that point that the manager noticed that Dexter had a thumb missing and asked him if he could indeed handle such work. Dexter told him that his missing thumb would not impede him in any way. Satisfied the manager told them to proceed.

Topsy-Turvy

The climb up the spiral stairway on the side of the vessel looked easy enough, but was actually quite arduous. Once at the top, they made their way to the troubled motor, which was fitted to a bracket at the edge of the vessel. Due to Dexter's disability, he would only be required to assist in lifting the heavy motor and Malcolm would do the intricate nuts and bolts work. Before they could see if the motor was indeed burnt out, the outer protection cover would have to be removed. Malcolm asked Dexter to pass him a 15mm spanner but, as it was being passed to him, it unfortunately slipped from his grasp. Malcolm made a valiant attempt to catch it, but overbalanced and fell down into the open hatch of the vessel. His downward plunge was suddenly halted when Dexter caught him by his wrist and shouted, "I've got you." He also shouted to those down below to come up and help him. Malcolm looked up and saw that Dexter was holding on to the guardrail, unfortunately with his left hand! Malcolm's body swung back and forth like a pendulum over the abyss of the hatchway and he could gradually feel Dexter's grasp weaken. He

118

looked up at Dexter, who looked directly into his eyes. He could see that Dexter was trying desperately to pull him back up, but without the locking power of his missing thumb, that task was proving to be impossible. Strange how life can often throw up these anomalous predicaments; the man Malcolm would have happily seen dead was now trying to save his life! However, it didn't take long for Dexter's weakness to be exposed and, slowly but surely, his grasp on Malcolm's wrist diminished. Malcolm could feel Dexter digging his nails into his wrist in a vain attempt to keep a hold of him until the others arrived. He could see the veins on the side of Dexter's head standing out with the effort, but Malcolm's fifteen stone weight proved too much for such a tenuous hold and he suddenly plunged downward into the suffocating yellow material.

Those still on the ground gasped in horror and quickly attempted to open the bottom access hatch. Unfortunately, this was rather a protracted process requiring the removal of a large number of bolts, but eventually they managed it. Once they had pulled the door fully open, the contents of the vessel flooded out into the room, scattering millions of small yellow granules across the floor and within minutes the room was inches deep in the material. By this time Dexter had joined them and assisted in scooping the remaining granules from the vessel. This also took an inordinate amount of time, but eventually they came upon Malcolm's body. His face was swollen and dark blue - an obvious sign of suffocation. An ambulance was sent for, but they told the controller it was not an emergency as the person was already dead.

During the time Malcolm had been employed he had attempted to settle his outstanding large debts, which left him with little to spend on anything other than essentials and certainly not on personal insurance. His burial would have been that of a pauper, but the Director's wife kindly paid for the burial plot adjacent to that of Victoria, thus fulfilling Malcolm's desire to be forever with his *inamorata*.

9. Just Cruising Along

Alice stretched her arms wide and closed her eyes, then raised her head to face the brilliant sunshine and lay back on her sun lounger in deep contentment. She was determined to acquire a suntan long before they had to return to cold, windy and rain-sodden old England. This was her third day on the "Sea Adventurer", which was now sailing through the still calm waters of the Caribbean. The ship was not one of those floating skyscraper types but was just large enough to contain a decent-sized swimming pool and, most importantly, an excellent selection of duty-free luxury shops.

Her husband Johnny had been trying to interest her in going on a cruise for several years, but she had always resisted, saying that cruising was only for one-foot-in-the-grave pensioners. But he persisted and in the end she relented, agreeing to fly out to the Bahamas to start the journey from there. It was only when she got on board that she found out just how sumptuous cruising was. The décor was fantastic, as was the food. She had never eaten so well in her life, and was astonished at both the quality and quantity of the meals. The diet she had been on for some time was totally forgotten as she continued to sample every type of delicacy on offer. She palliated her conscience by remembering that they had paid a lot of money to be on board so she was jolly well going to get her money's worth. She promised herself to work-off any extra weight when she got back home - meanwhile she intended to enjoy the cosseted lifestyle to the full.

Alice was amazed just how quickly she had got used to the luxurious manner of daily living. Exotic food, rivers of champagne, stewards at your beck and call, and on a whim, having her hair styled in various ways - even getting her toe nails manicured and painted, something she had always considered to be decadent if not downright silly. She thought about these things when once again she was occupying her favourite sun drenched spot on the open deck and was already planning a visit to the extensive and expensive shopping arcade. After an hour of topping up her tan, Alice made her way to a lift, which took her down the four decks to the shopping arcade. On leaving the lift, she accidentally caught her engagement ring on the metal doorway and, on examining it was dismayed to see that one of the stones had been dislodged, so she made her way to the nearest jewellers to see if they could repair it.

The jeweller told her that it was quite simple to repair and asked her if she would leave it with them, as they were very busy. He also pointed out that her gold wedding ring had a bad scratch on it and if she would like that attended to at the same time, they would be happy to do so. Alice told the shop assistant that the scratch had happened over a year ago when she scraped it on the garden wall. The assistant said that it was a pity to leave it that way as it could quite easily be polished out. The shop looked so expensive, with glass-fronted cases crammed with every conceivable luxury item, that she felt quite overawed. She also felt that the charge for having her rings attended to would be very expensive indeed. As if reading her mind, the assistant said that the shop did not charge for such minor repairs, so Alice left both rings in his care. Not wearing them felt strange, as they had never been off her finger during the past twelve years, so she felt disconcerted and uncomfortable not seeing them on her finger.

Alice's husband Johnny revealed that he was not the quite the seafaring type he had imagined himself to be, so he spent a considerable amount of time sealed up in his cabin feeling sorry for himself, just as most men do when they are only slightly ill. In consequence of this, Alice had to spend a fair amount of time on her own - not exactly the type of holiday excursion they had planned. Alice was a gregarious person so, when Johnny was not with her, she soon made friends with a good number of the other passengers. One in particular, a certain Max Lomax was a widower making this trip to fulfil a promise he had made to his departed wife. It appeared that they had always wanted to go on a cruise but somehow they had always been too busy to do so. As time progressed, Alice spent more and more time with him.

He was undoubtedly handsome, with greying hair, purposeful set mouth and good physique, but more importantly, as far as Alice was concerned, he had a wicked sense of humour, not unlike that of her own. Whenever they met, a large part of their time was spent in laughter. Mr. Lomax sometimes flirted with her. She found this amusing and flattering, until they met one night on the dimly lit foredeck he suddenly took hold of her and kissed her passionately! Initially she was shocked and started to resist, but the ardour of his kiss was such that her own sexuality was soon

123

inflamed and she responded with equal passion. They continued to embrace and kiss, then Alice suddenly came to her senses when Lomax suggested that they go to his cabin. She blurted out, "I'm a married woman!"

"I assumed that you were single, as you weren't wearing any rings!"

"My husband is in our cabin as he tends to get seasick quite often, I should have told you this earlier but I was so enjoying your company."

"And I most certainly am enjoying yours Alice, please stay, and I promise to behave myself."

Alice would have liked to have said yes, as it had been many, many years since she had felt so sensual and sexually aroused. Being aware of this made her afraid that she could not trust herself to resist any further advances from Lomax so she determinedly said, " I'm sorry Max" and made her way back to her cabin, feeling more than a little guilty.

During the days that followed Alice often saw Lomax as she walked around the ship and she studiously kept him at a distance, but he persisted in always being somewhere nearby, Alice was both charmed and flattered by his attentions, but equally alarmed by it. She even dreamt about the situation and, in some dreams, she would welcome Lomax's advances and willing give herself to him, while in others she would staunchly resist.

Alice was finding the cruise more and more stressful because of this situation. Even her husband, who was not noted for his perception of human behaviour started to say, "There's that same fellow again, he always seems to be around when we are!"

She decided that this was the time to take the bull by the horns and attempt to finalize the situation by replying, "Oh that's Max Lomax he is a very nice man, I often met him wandering around the deck when I went for a walk while you were laid up in bed."

She then recounted the story Lomax had related regarding his wife's last wishes.

"Poor fellow, how awful," Johnny said.

"Come on and I'll introduce you to him," she said walking towards Lomax, who on seeing her coming with husband close behind got ready to make a quick departure, but before he could do so Alice waved to him shouting, "Yoo Hoo, Max!"

He had no alternative but to wait, all the while wondering what was going to happen next. On reaching Lomax, Alice smiled at him and introduced her husband.

"Glad to meet you Max and thanks for the company you provided for Alice while I was laid-up," Johnny said to Lomax.

"I much appreciated her companionship, you are a very lucky man to have such a nice wife," Lomax replied, now somewhat relieved.

"I'm very much aware of that," Johnny said, looking at Alice and smiling.

Alice reciprocated his smile and was just about to say good-bye to Lomax when Johnny suddenly suggested that they retire to the lounge for a drink, which was the very last thing Alice wanted.

"We shouldn't monopolize Max's time, Johnny," she suggested, but Max turned to Johnny and said, "Thank you I'd like that very much."

Alice, standing behind her husband, scowled at Max, who returned the gesture by winking at her.

Once in the lounge, both men got on like a house on fire. In fact, as time progressed, Alice had the distinct impression that she was being sidelined and discovered that they had mutual interests in quite a few things. Little did Johnny realize that this also included his wife. Johnny asked to be excused to the little boys' room. As soon he had departed Max moved closer to Alice and his convivial persona evaporated. Alice had expected that he would now make some attempt to convince her to continue seeing him, but was more than surprised when he said, "Johnny is a very nice man, Alice and not at all what I had expected. It's obvious that he loves you very much - he is indeed a very fortunate man." Placing his hand on hers, he continued, "Don't worry Alice you will be seeing very little of me from now on." With that he gently kissed her hand and said, "I love you Alice, tell Johnny I was not feeling too great, which is positively true, and that I have gone to my cabin." With that he quickly departed.

Thereafter she only saw him at a distance. However, fate was to decree that this would not always be so and that Max was destined to play a further important part in her life in a way neither of them could have ever imagined.

Gradually Johnny was beginning to get the upper hand of his seasickness and spent more and more time with Alice. The ship moved out into deeper and less hospitable waters. The days flew past in seemingly endless dinner parties, wine tasting and gourmet appreciating events. During one of the all important sun tan sessions she fell asleep and dreamt that she was in love with a man whom she did not quite recognize - he was like Johnny yet also had similarities with Max. Part of his personality was quiet and attentive, the other bold and sensual. It was as if both these very different personalities had morphed into one. On waking, Alice usually remembered only snatched episodes of her dreams but she remembered all of this one which conveyed that her sub-conscience was telling her that Max had indeed found a place in her heart.

In the days following this revelation it was now Alice's turn to avoid coming into contact with Max. She was in a bit of a quandary as she had never been attracted to any man other than Johnny, who she had to admit was more than a little dull and pedestrian, yet was kind and attentive. She also had to admit that there were more than a few times when she would have liked to do something a bit out of the ordinary, like making love on the kitchen table rather than always in the darkness of the bedroom covered with the bedclothes. She suddenly thought that she could probably count on the fingers of one hand how many times she had seen her husband in the nude during the past twelve years of their marriage, and most of those had been accidental. Max on the other hand held out the possibility of exotic intimate interludes of unrestrained passion. The more she thought about Max the more her imagination took hold and the less inclined she was in avoiding him.

Eventually, Alice's physical desires overcame her innate rectitude and she started to make plans to 'accidentally' come into contact with Max. She had noticed for some time he regularly took an evening stroll along the deck just after dinner, so all she had to do was find some excuse to get Johnny out of the way. However, as things turned out that would not be a problem as Johnny said he was not feeling all that well and was off to bed. Now that the coast was clear Alice made a beeline for the upper deck with the high expectation of meeting Max and an equally high hope that her sexual imaginings would be fulfilled.

As soon as he saw Alice's face, Max knew that his suppressed longings and hopes were about to be realized. He rushed towards her, but before they could embrace, a sudden explosion ripped through the ship blowing them both overboard!

The impact of hitting the water and the shock of its coldness numbed each of them as they plunged beneath the waves. Alice involuntary swallowed some water and was immediately panic-stricken as she thought she was about to drown, but by sheer will power she held her breath and propelled herself upward. The sea was a mass of boiling turbulence. The ship was on fire in its mid section, lying on its side and sinking fast.

The noise of the creaking steel hull being torn apart, intermingled with the pitiful cries of drowning passengers was horrendous. Alice knew that she would have to get away from the sinking ship as soon as possible because the suction force when it went beneath the waves would draw her down with it. She swam as fast as she could, passing several bodies floating face down in the water. It all seemed so unreal, one moment sailing along in the lap of luxury, the next fighting for your life!

Alice had been sailing since the age of twelve and owned a four-metre boat, which she used whenever she went back to her parent's home in the Isle of Wight. She was not only well versed in seamanship but also had done a survival course, so she knew that her chances of surviving in such cold water was not very high. Contrary to popular belief, swimming made you lose body heat quicker, so she just lay still floating on the surface. After a short time, she started to shake violently - she knew this was the onset of hypothermia and if rescue did not come swiftly she would soon die. As she floated along she thought of Johnny and Max, wondering what had happened to them and also, how very short her own life had been, and all the things she had hoped to do in the coming years. Hypothermia was now taking firm control of her body and was gradually shutting down blood flow to her extremities - first her arms, quickly followed by her legs. In an attempt to maintain the circulatory system to the brain, she was now entering into a hallucinatory state and death was not far off.

A far-away voice disturbed Alice's hallucinations. She could hear her name being called out over and over again, and wanted to respond, but her brain was fully engaged in trying to remain alive, so she could not communicate in any way. Suddenly, strong arms grasped her roughly and pulled her upward into a boat. She was wrapped in a thermal blanket and felt a hand start to rub her face, arms and legs. These same arms picked her up and brought her into close intimate contact. At that particular moment, Alice did not care whose body it was just as long as they could transmit warmth to her. Just in time that life-giving heat started to restore her circulatory system, death had been averted.

When Alice's eyes finally came into focus, she was astonished and delighted to see Max smiling at her - it had been he who had snatched her from certain death. She wrapped her arms around him and kissed him warmly, but immediately asked about her husband. Max gave her the good news that he had seen him in another boat shortly after the ship sank, but they had quickly drifted apart because of the wave, which was created when the ship finally plunged into the depths. Alice asked Max if they were alone on the boat.

"I managed to pick out that young lad over there just before I saw you," Max replied, "he's quite badly injured."

Although Alice was not yet fully recovered, she made her way over to the bow where the young lad lay on a canvas sail. He looked about fifteen years of age and Alice's heart went out to him. She started to examine him. He appeared to be externally unmarked, which probably meant that he was injured internally, so may have been very near to the explosion. His eyes were glazed over and he looked to be in shock, and she noticed a small trickle of blood coming from the side of his mouth. Alice tried talking to him to see if he would respond, but he remained in the same insensible condition, clearly in a very bad way. Alice raised his head and placed a nearby life jacket under his head. Feeling she could do nothing more, she rejoined Max to help him search for other survivors.

Although they searched for some considerable

time they only encountered dead bodies, so they decided that it was fruitless and let the wind and tide carry them away from the disaster area. Max checked what was on board the boat. This consisted of approximately nine litres of water, tinned meat and fish, one thermal blanket, fishing tackle, a signal gun, a broken compass, a torch with dud batteries and a radar reflector with instructions on how to mount it at the top of the mast, so that any search planes or ships could more easily detect the boat. Now that they both had seen these provisions, they felt more secure in their belief that rescue would not be long in coming. Alice once again thought how ironic life could be, remembering that only a short while ago, her biggest problem was her love life.

Unfortunately for them, the one important thing they did not know was that the explosion had pulverized the ship's communications room before a mayday call could be sent out, so their chances of rescue were decidedly slim. They had no idea who the injured young man was and, as they searched his clothes for any ID, the flow of blood from his mouth continued unabated. Max and Alice settled down for the night huddled together for warmth and mutual assurance. They placed the injured youth between them so as to give him as much protection as possible and also hopefully a degree of warmth.

Max and Alice's long night was punctuated with periods of fitful sleep. Wakening in the early morning and looking out at an empty horizon and equally empty sky, there was still no sign of rescue. Max tried to cheer Alice up by saying that it took some time to organize a proper search operation and, until it arrived, they should make the best of it. Alice looked at the injured youth. Prior to settling down for the night, she had placed a piece of thick plastic above his head for some measure of protection from the sea spray. As she now removed it, she could clearly see that the poor lad had died. To make sure, she placed her hand on his neck and could feel it was icy cold, without a pulse. Max came to the same conclusion.

Initially, they covered the body up with the expectation that their rescuers would give the lad a decent burial, but as their situation moved into its third day with no sign of rescue and as the heat of the day increased, so too did the smell of the now fast decomposing flesh. What prompted them finally to come to a decision to push the corpse into the sea was their inability to eat anything while surrounded by the all-pervading noxious stench of the decomposing remains. The task was fraught with a mixture of disgust and sorrow. Although Max was a big man, he still required Alice to assist him in finally pushing "Tom" (they had christened the boy this as a means of respect) overboard. Max said a few words over the body they then lowered "Tom" to his rest. Instead of sinking, the body floated on the surface, because in their haste they had forgotten to weigh him down with something. They needn't have worried, because as they were still looking at the floating corpse, a large black fin cut through the water and headed straight towards it. The head of the shark broke the surface at high speed, grasped the body and plunged into the depths. The undertaker of the deep had solved their problem. Alice wondered how many more horrors they would they have to endure before rescue came, that was, if it ever did. This was the first time she had harboured doubts that they would ever see land again.

One of the more mundane and personal things, which very soon became apparent at the initial stage of being confined in such a small space, was the total lack of privacy, in particular when it came to heeding a call of nature. The only way that they could manage was to stick their bottoms over the side of the boat and do what they had to do. Initially Max had rigged-up a piece of canvas at the bow of the boat to give Alice a modicum of dignified cover, but this continually fell down and often at the most inconvenient and embarrassing moment. Eventually this was discarded, as it took too much effort to continually erect it, energy that they progressively did not have. In the end, they got used to performing their ablutions quite openly and have the sea splashing onto their posterior like a convenient bidet spray. The first time Max saw Alice in this preposterous position he burst out laughing and, like Queen Victoria, she was not amused. However as the old saying goes "They who laugh last, laugh the longest", and it was not much later when Max was in the same undignified position that he fell overboard and had to be rescued by a giggling Alice.

Rescue

"Alice!" Max suddenly shouted out, "We forgot to erect the radar deflector."

"What's a radar defibrillator?"

"No not a defibrillator, that's a machine for restarting a heart, what I mean is…." Max rushed over to the waterproof cabinet and took out the metal deflector and showed it to her.

"And what is a little piece of odd shaped metal going to do for us?"

"I'll tell you what this little odd shaped metal will do - it will deflect a rescue aircraft or ship's radar signal, which will pinpoint them to exactly where we are - that's what this little beauty will do for us!"

He threw his arms around her and shouting out joyfully, "Whoopee!"

Max quickly assembled the antenna mast, placed the radar beacon on top and hurriedly tied it in place. Almost as soon as they had completed this task, they heard the distant sound of aircraft engines. They reacted to this welcoming sound by kissing and hugging each other.

Both of them were so euphoric at the prospect of being rescued that they decided to celebrate by having a party, as they no longer had a reason to ration the water or food. Max pretended to be a waiter.

"Would madam like to refresh her hands?"

"Yes that would be very nice indeed."

Max poured water over her outstretched hands and asked her if she would like to order the wine. She in turn pretended to scrutinize the wine list.

"I think on this very special occasion, I'll have a bottle of your best champagne."

As Max poured her a large cupful of water, Alice shouted out, "I can hear the aircraft engines coming closer!" Both of them listened intently. "Yes, yes, I

134

can hear it getting louder, oh what a beautiful sound," she said excitedly, pointing in a westerly direction. "Look Max, its high up over there."

"Yes I see it!"

At that precise moment, on board the search aircraft, the radar engineer suddenly saw a signal deflection blip on his radar screen, which disappeared before he could lock on to its co-ordinates. The radar deflector had not been properly secured to the mast and had fallen off.

Both Alice and Max witnessed this heart-stopping event and watched helplessly as the deflector bounced onto the wooden deck and was catapulted into the sea!

Both of them were struck dumb by the enormity of this tragedy and their only hope now lay in the possibility that the aircraft had picked up their signal. They watched spellbound as the aircraft turned back to their direction. Alice shouted out, "They've seen us Max, they've seen us!"

On board the aircraft the radar operator said, "Sorry Captain, I was sure I saw something," and the Captain replied, "We're getting low on fuel, so I'm heading back to base." Max and Alice watched dejectedly as the plane flew out of sight.

Both of them had been so fixated on the aircraft that they had failed to notice that the water container had toppled over and most of its contents had escaped onto the blood stained deck. In those few premature ecstatic moments of heightened exuberance, their chances of survival had been drastically reduced. They had a most uncertain and possibly tragic future.

Alice and Max now faced the prospect of dying of thirst long before anyone could come to their aid, consequently they would have to conserve as much water as they could, which meant very strict rationing indeed. That few moments of fun had inadvertently cost them dearly. Alice looked at Max and said, "I'm scared Max." He wrapped his arms around her and said, "Don't be, I'm sure it won't be long before we are rescued," but there was little conviction in his voice. Now they could only hope that the search for survivors would not be called off.

"I was just looking at this boat we are in - don't you think it is rather a strange type of craft to have on a cruise liner?" Alice suddenly said to Max, who cast his eye around it.

"To me a boat is a boat, what's different about it."

"It's a sailboat, it's much too small to act as a lifeboat," Alice replied.

She examined the boat in more detail and soon found a small brass plaque screwed to a foredeck scuttle, which read "To Captain McBride for twenty years of faithful service". Underneath on another brass plate was inscribed the name of the boat "Codswallop". Obviously, the boat had been a gift from the shipping company and Alice wondered if the Captain had not been too enamoured with the gift and had shown his displeasure by naming the boat in this derisory way. Alice probed around other small cabinets at the bow hoping to find anything further which might enhance their chances of survival. She came upon two watertight plastic containers, which contained pictures of the Captain of the "Sea Adventurer" with his wife and children, and others of him sailing in the "Codswallop". On the back of one was written "Malta" and on another "Venice".

As Alice looked, she wondered if the Captain's wife was now a widow. Max saw Alice looking at the pictures and said dispassionately, "Get rid of those and use the plastic containers as bailing buckets."

She did as he suggested but couldn't bring herself to throw the pictures away, and bundled them together, placing them back into the rear of the cabinet and securing the door firmly. In the circumstances, it was a futile gesture but she felt compelled to do it.

During the day, the sun beat down on them mercilessly while at night they shivered with cold as the sea spray intermittently rained down on them. They took it in turn to use the plastic buckets to bail out the water from the bottom of the boat. These conditions gradually sapped both their energy and resolve, added to which, the drinking water was almost gone. Alice looked at Max, noting that his skin was red from the searing heat of the sun and his lips were cracked and bleeding from lack of water. She put her hand to her mouth and felt it was similarly cracked and that her hair was thick with salt spray. Both of them were in a bad way: dehydration had set in. Although they had enough dried food, what they badly needed was water. Alice dreamed about water every time she fell asleep - drinking it, swimming in it, washing her matted and tangled hair – and, sometimes hallucinating that she was still living the pampered life on board the "Sea

Adventurer", only to wake to the harsh reality of their continuing dire situation. Initially she cried a lot, but as Max pointed out, this was achieving nothing other than losing even more precious fluids.

The boat had been stocked with a good amount of tinned food, fruit, meat and fish. Alice noted that they had all passed their sell by dates, not that this would have worried her or Max. Unfortunately, the survival rations did not include a tin opener! They tried every method, including bashing it on the side of the boat, but the only thing this achieved was damaged woodwork. They hit the cans together, but this only dented the tins without puncturing them. There was nothing on board strong or sharp enough to penetrate them. It was highly frustrating to think that only a thin layer of steel separated them from the life-giving contents of those stupid tins. Although their little boat had been a lifesaver, it was also their floating prison and possibly their eventual coffin.

Singing in the Rain

As they huddled together asleep one night under the cover of the mast canvas, Max was suddenly woken by the sound of torrential rain battering down into the boat. He quickly shook Alice awake and gave out a great whoop of joy. She soon joined him in this chorus of jubilation. Both of them put their heads backward and opened their mouths wide to welcome the life saving liquid into their body. Suddenly Max shouted to Alice that the rain might stop at any moment, so they should try to save as much of it as possible. Max quickly got hold of the now empty water container and Alice formed a funnel from the metallic thermal blanket and channelled the pouring rain into the container. Although it was raining hard, it still took some time to totally fill the water casket. Almost as soon as this was done, the rain stopped. Neither of them were religious, but both looked skyward and chorused a loud thank you to the now cloudless sky.

They both had a natural strong desire to drink their fill right away, but remembered reading the small booklet in the survival equipment, which cautioned against drinking too much water after prolonged abstinence and advised using only small quantities initially, as too much liquid could drastically effect the internal organs. It was agonizing just taking little sips of water when your body was crying out for great gulps of it. By the next day they had regained a lot of their normal functionality, so much so that Max was more like his old joking self and when Alice said to him, "I'd love to have a bath."

"Shall I run it for you madam?" he replied, bowing.

"That would be most kind of you, my good man."

"Think nothing of it madam."

With that he pushed a startled Alice overboard! Once she had bobbed to the surface, Max shouted to her, "Is the water temperature right for madam?"

"I'll madam you when I get out of here," she said scowling back at him.

She then realized that the water was indeed at a nice temperature, so forgetting Max's joking, she relaxed and swam around for a while, enjoying the cleansing effect of the water, but her enjoyment was cut short by Max shouting, "I take it your coming back on board?"

"I'll think about it," she replied, but suddenly saw Max's face change expression from teasing fun to one of sheer horror.

"Alice swim as fast as you can, move yourself, quickly, quickly!"

She instinctively looked around and to her horror saw a black dorsal fin cutting swiftly through the surface of the water and heading directly towards her - undoubtedly it was a shark!

Adrenaline is secreted in our body from our ancestral distant past. It was there to help us escape the clutches of predators, that is, until we became the supreme predator. Now that same chemical was being massively pumped into Alice's veins and explosively increased the power of her muscles. She now cut through the water at a speed far above anything Olympian swimmers could achieve, but this was no match for the king of the sea, which within seconds had flashed past her and mysteriously stopped between her and the boat totally blocking her escape. Alice froze with fear. Max was equally traumatized and unable to think what to do. All of a sudden the dolphin's head popped out of the water and, making that peculiar squeaky sound, looked cheekily at Alice as it slowly glided towards her.

Every part of Alice's body was in pain following her supreme effort. The dolphin came close enough so that she could touch it and she said, "You silly old bugger you scared the life out of me."

As the sea was dead calm, Max said he'd like to join Alice in the water so that he could also have a 'bath'. What he didn't tell her that this was necessary because he had wet himself during the traumatic moments before they realised that it was a dolphin.

Faux Pas

Having fresh water also meant they could soften the concrete-like survival biscuits, which until now were totally inedible. Consequently, life became more bearable, their health began to improve and their blistered, cracked skin started to heal. Most days nothing was sighted, except for the occasional high-flying aircraft, but from time to time they came close to whales and shoals of dolphins, on one occasion the gigantic fifty tonne blue whale. The dolphins were always welcome, as their playful nature tended to lift their spirits, but as suddenly they made their appearance, they would just as quickly depart.

One day, as Max was taking a swim, Alice saw the usual dark fin of a dolphin cut through the water at speed and head in the direction of their boat. She suddenly became aware that the dorsal fin was much, much larger and thicker than that of a dolphin! This time, it was undoubtedly a shark and was gathering speed for an attack on Max. Alice screamed at him to get out of the water. Unfortunately he thought she was just fooling around, until he heard her screaming, "Shark, shark!"

Max struck out for the boat with all his might. Although this was a natural reaction, it would have been better if had he stopped swimming and floated on the surface of the water, because it is movement that attracts the shark and leads to it attacking.

Throughout all this commotion Alice continued screaming, "Faster Max, faster!"

Max reached the boat in time for Alice to grab his forearms and begin helping him into the boat, but just then he gave out a massive, agonizing scream as the shark clamped its jaws onto his legs. Alice could feel him being pulled back into the sea. Max held tenaciously onto the side of the boat with a vice like grip while Alice dug her fingers into his skin. Suddenly, the pulling ceased and Alice watched in horror as the sea turned blood red. The thrashing of the shark also ceased and the sea once again was calm. The shark had gone. It was not until Alice had helped the screaming Max fully into the boat that she saw with horror that he no longer had any legs! The shark had bitten off both just below his hips and blood was now gushing from the torn and ragged remains, filling the bottom of the boat. The trauma and the adrenalin inhabiting Max's body mercifully acted as an analgesic and helped to numb his agonizing pain. His mind was totally overwhelmed and befuddled, and Max had no idea that he had lost his legs and would die very soon.

Although Alice was equally traumatized, she was also well aware that she was about to lose Max. She felt like screaming in her inability to help him, but restrained herself and pulled part of the canvas sail over the lower half of his body. Max was sinking fast as he held out his hand towards her and said, "Alice I'm so very, very cold."

Those were the last words he was to utter as his body trembled violently then suddenly went limp. Max was dead. Alice bent forward and kissed his cold lifeless face before letting out an ear-shattering scream. She was now totally alone on a vast sea with little or no prospect of being rescued. It was only a matter of time until it was her turn to die, the only question was by what means.

Horror on Horror

Alice covered up Max as best she could by pulling the rest of the sail over him, all the while walking through his blood, which was sloshing around the bottom of the boat. She stoically set about dredging Max's blood out of the boat with the plastic bailing bucket, but twice she had to stop to vomit over the side. Eventually she completed the grim, nauseating task and spent a considerable time crying. Then, to cap it all, the temperature fell and it started to rain heavily. That night was terrifying for Alice - as well as the rain, the wind picked up, tossing the boat each and every way, moving Max's body back and forth. Alice had to cover him up time and time again, as she could not bear to look at his mangled corpse. The horrors she had to suffer in this small boat seemed to be never ending.

The morning brought much better weather with bright sun and calm waters, but this had little effect on Alice's outlook, as there was still no sign of a rescue ship or aircraft, plus Max's crumpled body still occupied the bow of the boat. Alice knew that, sooner or later, she would have to push Max's deteriorating body into the sea. She tried not to think about it, hoping that a rescue ship would come along and take that awful, horrific responsibility from her.

143

The temperature throughout the day rose higher and higher. The next day got even warmer. She started to think of ways of lifting Max's considerable weight over the side of the boat, but still hoped upon hope that a miracle would happen and that it wouldn't be necessary. The next day proved to be even warmer and, by this time, Max's body had started to putrefy. The sickly stench of decomposing flesh hung heavily in the air. Alice decided she had no alternative but to set about pushing the corpse into the sea, the only question was how. Max had been quite a large person and she could not think of anything on board that would assist her to get the body over the side, but she would have to try.

She approached Max's body with more than a degree of trepidation, and each step she took towards him the stronger was the stench of decomposition. Alice had to turn back twice as she retched and vomited. Finally, she tore part of her skirt, put it around her mouth and made a new attempt at the grisly task. On lifting the canvas cover off Max, she was totally overcome by the horror of his distorted, festered and rotting face, but she knew she had to complete the task come what may.

First, she attempted to slide his body nearer the edge of the boat, but was only partially successful, then she spotted the grappling rod used to pull the boat closer to its berth. She placed this under the body and, bit-by- bit, levered it up over the side but she could not manage to get it very far. Alice took a rest and went to the other end of the boat to get a breath of comparatively fresh air. She stayed there for some time trying to think of some other means of lifting his corpse into the sea, then her eye alighted on a propane gas cylinder and she thought - if I could attach that to the corpse and fling it overboard - there was a good chance that it might be heavy enough to drag the body down with it. As no other option presented itself, she set about organizing the sickening task.

Alice poked around once again in the numerous cupboards and was more than relieved to discover several pieces of sturdy rope. She took a length and attached it to the cylinder and, putting on her mask once more, made her way towards the stern. Once there she stopped to think where it would be best to place the rope to provide maximum grip so that when she pushed the cylinder overboard, the rope wouldn't come lose. There was only one horrifying place that would suffice - the neck! Being in such close proximity to Max's rotting body and touching his clothes had been bad enough, but the thought of now grasping his head was proving a step too far. She spent some time contemplating the terrible task ahead and, time after time, she could not bring herself to carry it out. She decided to carry it out under the cover of darkness and, when the sun had fully set, Alice motivated herself and moved once again back towards the corpse. Once in position she touched the top of Max's head, swiftly placed the noose around it and quickly kicked the cylinder overboard. The effect was immediate - Max's body was catapulted the final short distance over the edge of the boat and was dragged down into the depths of the sea. Alice felt guilty that she had not thought about saying a prayer or something before she kicked the cylinder overboard, however the grisly task had been completed and that was the main consideration. She once again set about cleaning the boat by pouring in buckets of sea water then bailing it out again, until eventually the boat looked and smelt a lot sweeter. Now that Alice was totally alone, she thought about all that had transpired during the time she had been adrift and how much she had changed, from being a pampered lady of leisure aboard a luxury cruise liner with the only thing on her mind being how to improve her sex life, to acting as a funeral director having to dispose of a horrifically pulverized and contaminated corpse. Surely Alice thought, things could not get any worse. How wrong she was.

A Gift from the Sea

Due to both the mental and physical strains Alice had endured the previous day, she slept like a top, but was suddenly woken by a loud scraping noise. It was only when her eyes came into focus that she noticed that the boat was in the shade of something nearby. Her heart leapt at the thought that it was a rescue ship, but sadly on looking up she saw, to her amazement, that it was a giant steel shipping container. She remembered reading about the huge number of these containers that have been washed overboard from container ships and were now bobbing about in the seas of the world, probably about ten thousand. The container continued to scrape the side of her boat and Alice began to be afraid that it might cause damage or even sink her little craft, so she started to make preparations to move away from it. Half way through this task she suddenly had a thought - what if it contained something that might be useful in helping her survive, like food or bottled water. The container was floating on its side, which would make any attempt to open the doors just that little bit easier. Alice manoeuvred her boat close to the container doors and was delighted to see that, when it had broken free from the ship's deck, the door security lock had been torn off. Now all that was required was to release the sliding bolts, but this would require some muscle power or a good hammer, both of which were in short supply. It was going to be quite a dangerous task, as the waves continued to buffet the huge container against the boat. Almost as if it were an answer to her unspoken prayers the wind abated and the buffeting from the container ceased, so now was the chance for Alice to try to gain access to that rusting hulk and, hopefully, its life saving contents.

Alice looked around the boat for anything that she could use as a hammer, but was unable to find anything suitable, until she saw the boat hook used to clasp onto a mooring buoy. It was more than long enough, with a large metal hook at one end and, in some ways it was almost better than a hammer, as the hook could lift the security bolts to the right position for opening the latch. Then all she would have to do was slide the bolt to the open position and the doors would release their contents into her waiting arms. Alice set to it with a vengeance, prodding, poking and thumping the bolt for all she was worth, yet without any tangible success. She laboured on through the heat of the day, hour after hour, until slowly but steadily the top bolt started to move, then suddenly with a loud bang, it moved fully back. Alice celebrated this accomplishment by taking a well-earned rest. She started to tackle the remaining bolt, but by this time the boat hook was showing very distinct signs of wear and Alice was fearful that it might break before she was able to release the last bolt. Her worst fears were realized when the metal point of the hook broke off. She was distraught that all her hard work had come to naught and was so angry that she hit the bolt with the remaining wooden shaft. The bolt slid to the open position, the container doors flew open and the contents showered out into the sea. Box after box bobbed around the boat, hundreds and hundreds of them. Alice gave out a whoop of joy, did a little dance of pleasure and hurriedly scooped one into the boat before the waterlogged cardboard box had a chance to sink. Clearly stamped on the outside of the box were the words "Manicure sets. Made in China".

Alice stared at them in disbelief and hurriedly tore the box open, tipping its contents into the bottom of the boat, which revealed they were indeed cheap manicure sets. She fished another box out of the sea and opened it, but it also contained the same low quality instruments. The irony was not lost on her as she contrasted the contents of those silly boxes with her present precarious position. Alice screamed at the sky, then fell down sobbing into the bottom of the boat and, totally exhausted, curled herself into a foetal position and fell asleep. When she awoke, the container with its precious contents had sunk without trace, leaving her once again alone on that vast sea.

If Only

Alice decided to wash her clothes to rid them of any last traces of contamination. As she only possessed one pair of panties, a bra, a torn skirt and a ragged blouse, washing would not be an arduous task. Once she had done this she took a quick dip in the sea, holding onto the side of the boat and keeping a sharp lookout for marauding sharks.

She set up a clothesline and lay down to await their drying. As she lay there naked, she thought back to the time when her husband had suggested that they have a holiday at a nudist colony. At the time she thought she would have been quite happy to try it, but her innate modesty prevailed and they went to Blackpool instead! Lying there, she suddenly heard the distinct sound of an aircraft engine and immediately jumped to her feet, running forward to where the Vary flare pistol was kept.

She grabbed it, loaded a cartridge and, holding it aloft, pulled the trigger. Nothing happened, so she pulled the trigger again and again, still without result. By this time the aircraft was almost directly overhead.

"I'm here, I'm here. Over here you idiots!" Alice shouted and waved.

The plane continued northwards and, in a few moments, was out of sight. It was only at that point that she realized that she had forgotten to take the safety-catch off. She also realized that she had been completely naked when she was trying to attract the aircrew's attention, not that she cared a fig about that. Once her clothes had dried, Alice decided not to bother wearing them and continued on her fateful journey *au naturel*.

Modus Operandi

Alice tried to remember how long she had been at sea but could not do so as each day seemed like any other. The sun came up and you searched the horizon from end to end, and did likewise with the sky, then checked that the boat hadn't taken on any water. If it had, you bailed it out, then soaked a survival biscuit in rain water for ten minutes during which you heeded your routine call of nature. Then you tackled the survival biscuit, pretending that it is actually something edible. And so the days progressed.

One would have thought that night would be the quietest of times, not so as Alice found out, especially when a whale was in the vicinity - the sound of its blowhole in close proximity was indeed memorable. Then there were the numerous types of bird making their annual pilgrimage. As she listened to them flying overhead, Alice envied them; they knew where they were going and had the freedom to do it, unlike her who had no idea where she was. She could only hope that she was being carried along on a strong current, which would bring her ever nearer to civilization and, ultimately, rescue.

The vicissitudes of Life

One day while Alice was taking an afternoon siesta, she was suddenly woken by the sound of a passing ship, a large fuel tanker flying an unrecognisable flag. Alice immediately jumped up and started to wave frantically at some crew on board, who waved just as enthusiastically back at her.

Her first reaction was to think that her days adrift were now over, but as she looked at the ship, she realized that it was not stopping and that some of the crew were actually taking pictures of her! Were they mad, could they not see she was in distress?

Then realization suddenly hit her, she was so used to being naked that she had totally forgotten about it, so when the crewmembers saw her they had thought she was some lone sailor and who was tantalizing them with her nudity.

"You stupid, idiotic, chauvinist clowns - why don't you let your brains do the thinking sometime instead of that other part of your anatomy!" Alice shouted after them.

It was only when the ship was a considerable distance from her that she remembered the distress pistol, but thought better of using it as by now the crew would probably be fully occupied leering at the pictures they had taken of her, so firing the pistol would only be a waste of a good shell. Still, it was heartbreaking watching rescue disappear over the horizon.

Facebook to the Rescue

The days drifted past slowly. Alice felt as if she was a prisoner in solitary confinement awaiting her turn for execution. The food had almost gone and it hadn't rained for some considerable time, so water was now also becoming an issue. To break the monotony and, as she was tired of the oppressive heat of the day, Alice decided to have a bath. Looking around to see if there was any sign of a shark, she slid into the water.

She immediately felt better and splashed around clinging onto the side of the boat. Just as she was about to get back into the boat, she suddenly felt something brush gently against her right leg. Almost immediately she could feel a stinging sensation which increased in intensity by the second and, by the time she had pulled herself back on board, her leg had started to pain her as it turned bright red. Within minutes she lay on the floor of the boat writhing in agony. She had unfortunately come into contact with a jelly fish, and not just any old jelly fish but the Portuguese man-of-war - one of the most innocuous looking creatures in the sea, but also one of the most dangerous. It's extremely painful stings produces shock-like sensations, intense joint and muscle pain, vomiting and even hysteria. Alice was in a bad way and needed immediate treatment.

She slipped into a trance-like state and felt herself being lifted up and carried aloft, wondering if this was how some people felt when they were entering death. The sudden prick of an injection needle into her arm brought her out of her reverie and she saw that she was in a hospital! Still unsure if what she was seeing was real or not, she was just about to say something when a man wearing a military uniform brought his face close to her and said, "Take it easy, you're safe now. You're on board HMS Sword, we got to you just on time. Now just lie back while I examine you."

Alice would have loved to have shouted out, "I have been saved, I have been saved, I have been saved!" She attempted to lift her head, but was too weak. She lay back in the clean, soft, crisp bed sheets and gently fell asleep as the injections started to take effect.

"Gunnery crew ready sir."

"Open fire," the Captain gave the order and two four-inch shells tore into the "Balderdash", quickly sending it to the bottom. As it sank, the Captain said to his fellow officer, "What a shame Number One, that was a fine looking vessel."

"But as you said sir, we had to do it as it would certainly be a danger to other shipping.

The Captain asked if there had been any reply from the Admiralty regarding their rescued lady.

"Yes sir. It appears that our passenger might be a certain Mrs. Alice Winterton, who was a passenger on that cruise ship that went down over two months ago." The Captain looked startled.

"Good Lord, you mean to say that fragile little creature was on her own all that time!"

The reason for the warship being able to find Alice was because the fuel tanker crew had posted her naked pictures on Facebook. They got over a million hits. Alice's husband had been informed about the pictures and contacted the authorities, and the rest, as they say, is history. She was reunited with her husband and, after a period of recuperation, she wrote a best-selling book about her ordeal entitled "Codswallop, the Sea and Me". She also found time to inaugurate and run a local nudist group.